Gun Fury

Veteran gunfighter Tom Dix and his pal Dan Shaw get a telegraph message from the remote border town of Gun Fury. Both men know that it must be serious for their friend Wild Bill Hickok to contact them. They saddle up and ride knowing that something perilous is brewing.

Death awaits and greets them as soon as they reach Gun Fury. Within hours bodies start to pile up. And the curious thing is that the infamous Hickok claims he never sent for them.

Trapped, Dix and Shaw have to fight for their lives in Gun Fury.

Gun Fury

WALT KEENE

A Black Horse Western

ROBERT HALE · LONDON

ISBN 978-0-7090-8779-3

Robert Hale Limited
Clerkenwell House
Clerkenwell Green
London EC1R 0HT

www.halebooks.com

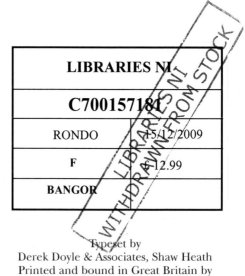

Typeset by
Derek Doyle & Associates, Shaw Heath
Printed and bound in Great Britain by
CPI Antony Rowe, Chippenham and Eastbourne

Dedicated to Jackie Autry and
the memory of her Cowboy.

PROLOGUE

Few men died of old age in the Wild West. Life was usually shorter than it was back East, but far more eventful across the merciless land which was growing bigger with every new day that had the nerve to dawn. Some men achieved brief glory and some have remained infamous to the present day. Heroes and villains came in various shapes and sizes. Sometimes the baby-faced innocent youngster hid a monster with no morality flowing through his veins. Often the most hideous of scarred faces disguised a man with a heart of gold. Women who had the most beautiful of appearances were often brutal killers and even the kindly grandmother could not be trusted not to blow the back of your head off with a hidden gun.

So many people of so many shades roamed the West.

Men who were clad in the best of clothing with the most expensive hand-tooled shooting rigs and who proclaimed themselves to be gunslingers often found themselves faced by someone with holes in their pants and a gun hanging from a leather lace. Yet the speed of the hands and the accuracy of placing bullets in opponents had nothing to do with fashion.

Showdowns were won by those who did it better. It mattered nothing at all what you looked like when it came to drawing metal from leather and fanning a gun hammer.

Only a few were recognizable for what they truly were. Some men honed their look to match their reputation. Some men had their reputations exaggerated by writers bent on making money out of the West and those who inhabited its vast untamed regions.

Some men, though, were exactly what they looked like.

They were legends in their own lifetimes. Sometimes being a legend is hard to live up to. It can destroy you as easily as a bullet. For men eventually grow old if their luck holds.

Being a man was never easy in the West.

Being branded as a legend was even tougher.

So it was with one man who was everything his legend made him out to be. Even though he had many vices, he was probably more heroic than was claimed in any of the tall stories of his life.

Soon the man and the legend would be tested.

There was nowhere to hide.

But even at their lowest ebb some men find the strength and courage not to hide. Even when death looms over them, they stand up and are counted.

ONE

The weathered wooden marker rocked in the stony ground as an unseen prairie breeze moved tumbleweed across its vast expanse towards the remote town. The words on the board had faded since it had last been painted. Now only the marks of the brush strokes could be seen. Gun Fury. Population 1,228. Elevation 34 feet. It seemed that no one had corrected the words since the town's decline. Yet this did not mean a thing to the handful of riders who steered their mounts towards the settlement of sun-bleached buildings. They knew the name of the town and did not need reminding. They had been here many times before and to them it was a place where they knew they would be able to spend the month's cowboy wages which was already burning holes in their pockets. Set in a landscape devoid of anything remotely green the town had gone downhill quickly since its glory days.

The horses carefully stepped over the rusting rail tracks and passed the disused cattle pens close to the small railroad depot. The town's children had made short work of smashing every pane of glass in the windows of the now derelict structure. The seven horsemen closed the distance between themselves and the nearest of the buildings. A few of the grubby children stood beside the depot with rocks in their hands and stared at the cowboys who rode slowly against a backdrop of distant mountains. With the sun almost directly overhead, each of the riders looked as though he had been stained in shadow. Dust kicked up around the hoofs of the untrimmed saddle horses and floated in the same direction as the tumbleweed.

The children turned and ran towards the town to inform the saloon keepers of the imminent arrivals. Each child knew that they would be given a penny for their trouble.

At one time cowboys had filled the streets of Gun Fury most days of the year as one herd followed another to the railhead on the outskirts of town. Now only cowboys from the few remaining ranches across the range visited. Half the buildings along Main Street were boarded up. Those which remained open were ones such as hung on until the end of every town. One brothel now had to cater for the needs of the menfolk where once a dozen had prospered. Saloons now dominated. One bank, a café, one general store and a barber shop managed to continue surviving as well as the livery stable at the end of the long thoroughfare. A feed store still had enough patrons to keep going but that was about it. Apart from the marshal's office set close to the bank, which still boasted a law officer and his deputy, no other businesses had survived.

Gun Fury had certainly seen better days. Perhaps it would again but none of the remaining 300 souls who still lived within its unmarked boundaries believed it. They had prospered when the railhead had been opened and that had seen the town boom and treble in size, but three years later a new spur had been laid fifty miles to the south. The trail herds had seen their long journeys reduced. They no longer came.

Gun Fury was dying.

Soon it would become just another sand-swept ghost town. Yet those who populated it now liked the fact that few outsiders came. To some it made the town a perfect place in which to dwell.

During the previous year strangers had started to drift into the remote settlement from all four corners of the big country that surrounded it. These men were unlike those who had established the original town. Hard work was not to their liking. They did not want a place to work or set up business. They wanted somewhere to spend their ill-gotten gains.

A sanctuary from the law.

But Gun Fury was not ideal because it still had a marshal and a deputy. That could be dealt with, though.

The Golden Spur was the largest of the five saloons dotted along Main Street. It had been completed just before the railroad managers had decided to stop running locomotives into the remote town. It still looked good but, like everything else in Gun Fury it would soon start to decay.

Although it boasted two bar rooms only one remained open. This long room had flocked red and gold imported paper on its walls. Satin drapes hung at its corners and the card tables still had baize upon them. A mahogany bar counter went the twenty-eight feet length of the room but now only the owner worked behind it. The days of five bartenders working alongside one another had gone, even for the Golden Spur.

Inside the saloon the morning sun clashed with the dust and the low-hanging cigar smoke as it cascaded through the three tall windows. Eight local men were seated in the room, playing poker at two tables. But it was not to them that the barman kept returning his attention. It was the figure who had been in town for more than a month and had done nothing except pull the corks on one whiskey bottle after another.

In a corner with his back to the wall the gaunt figure sat. He had hooded eyes and a sallow complexion. It was obvious that he had not set foot out in the daylight for as long as he had been in Gun Fury and he seemed to have no desire to do so. His long flowing hair and drooping moustache seemed to be from another time. A time when mountain men roamed this land, but this was no mountain man. His trail gear was worn and looked as tired as he did himself. There seemed to be no spark left in the once flamboyant character. He poured another shot of whiskey into the tumbler and downed the fiery liquid in one swift movement.

It was obvious to everyone in Gun Fury that he was drunk but no one with brains had the guts to mention it. Yet even a reputation for being one of the deadliest gunfighters the West had ever spawned would not keep the naïve at bay for ever. Not when they saw the volume of whiskey the man was consuming.

For even in his sorry condition he was still a man whose very name commanded respect. Most of the time, that was.

The man with a white apron tied around his middle walked from behind the bar counter with a fresh bottle in his hand. He headed straight to the long-haired customer, who stared at his empty glass the way most men would stare at the body of a loved one.

The hooded eyes looked up. They seemed lifeless and dulled.

'Rufas!'

'Fresh bottle, Wild Billy,' the barman said, placing the new one down and picking up the empty. 'Ya want me to get my wife to rustle ya up some vittles? This stuff will burn a hole in even the hardiest of guts without some skillet grease to slow it up a tad.'

James Butler Hickok reached for the bottle and pulled its cork with his teeth. He spat it at the closest spittoon. He did not miss.

'Thank you kindly, Rufas,' Hickok nodded. 'A little broth maybe and some bread. I don't hanker for any grease right now.'

The barman smiled as he picked up the coin which had awaited his arrival. 'I'll get it for ya.'

'You are a gentleman, Rufas.'

Rufas Hardy smiled and returned to his bar.

Hickok blinked hard in a vain attempt to see clearly. His eyes were playing tricks with him again and he did not like it. He wondered if it were the liquor or the old problem which had dogged him for the previous three years.

He poured another glassful of the amber liquor and smiled at it. He lifted it up, navigated the glass under his moustache to his mouth and swallowed.

Then a noise beyond the hanging drape close to the saloon hall drew his attention. It was the sound of men laughing out loud. Hickok turned his head and saw three men enter the room to his left. He screwed up his eyes but it was useless. He could not clearly make out the new arrivals.

They were just shadows in the sunlight: blurred images made no clearer by the whiskey.

Hickok raised a glass as if in greeting to them.

He could hear their barely concealed amusement as they walked to the counter, rested their hands upon its polished surface and spurred boots upon its brass rail. They were not townsfolk, Hickok told himself. They were probably cowboys if they wore spurs.

James Butler Hickok hated cowboys.

'Ya still drinking, Wild Bill?' a husky voice from one of the trio asked. 'Don't ya do nothin' 'cept drink?'

Hickok forced himself to nod. 'Indeed.'

'I heard tell that ya all washed up, Bill,' another of the men said with a laugh.

Hickok inhaled deeply. There was a time when he would have killed anyone for mocking him or his abilities. But that had been before time had caught up with him. He refilled the glass and stared at it with eyes unable to focus.

'Is that true, Wild Bill?' the first voice asked out loud. 'Are ya all washed up? Maybe ya ought to go to the barber shop and get yaself a trim. That mane sure looks awful heavy for an old man to carry on his back.'

'Crying shame!' another voice added. 'I used to read all them stories about him in them dime novels. Look at him now! Just an old drunk!'

'Maybe them stories were just a lotta eyewash, boys.'

'Yeah! Made up for folks back East to swallow.'

Angrily, James Butler Hickok placed the glass down on the wet table and abruptly stood up to his full height. His hooded eyes burned across the saloon at the three men like a pair of branding-irons. He was swaying but was still a formidable sight to anyone with brains. Even drunk he still looked dangerous. His matched pair of Army Colts were in their custom made holsters as they had always been. Their ivory grips poked out above his belt buckle as if waiting for the most famous exponent of the cross draw to drag them clear and start shooting.

'You wanna repeat them words?' Hickok asked in a low whisper. 'I'd hate to kill you three because I misheard.'

The three men remained silent.

The tall figure walked around the table and plucked up the whiskey bottle. He dropped it into the left side pocket of his long-fringed jacket, then paused for a moment. His expression was as grim as any of the photographic images he had sat for during his colourful life.

'I could kill all three of you and get away with it,

boys,' Hickok said coldly. 'No jury ever found old Wild Bill guilty even when I was. C'mon! Go for them hoglegs and try your luck.'

The barman ran around the counter across the room to the side of Hickok.

'I'll take ya up to ya room, Wild Billy,' he muttered. 'Ya tired. Bessie will bring up ya grub in a few minutes.'

Hickok glanced away from the blurred images across the room to the small Rufas Hardy. He nodded.

'Much obliged, Rufas,' said.

The thin swaying figure leaned on the barman and was guided beyond the long drapes to the carpeted staircase which led up to half a dozen rooms. At one time there had been a waiting list to stay at the Golden Spur, but now Hickok was the only guest.

'I thought ya was gonna kill them *hombres* for sure, Bill,' Rufas said in a hushed tone.

'I was just bluffing, Rufas,' Hickok admitted. 'I'd hate to shoot up your bar.'

'With that skill at bluffin' ya oughta sit in on a poker game or two.' The man helped Hickok up the staircase.

'It's a tad early, Rufas.' Hickok nodded. 'Maybe later.'

The three cowboys began to laugh again as they sipped on their suds at the bar counter. They had managed to control their amusement until they were sure the famed gunfighter was out of range.

They might have been simple cowpunchers but they were not suicidal.

TWO

A million stars sparkled against a black sky like precious diamonds on a velvet cloth above the vast range. The heat had gone along with the sun hours earlier yet neither of the riders noticed. They had at last found the town that they had been searching for.

Their goal was in view.

Gun Fury was a welcome sight even from out on the range. The flickering coal-tar lights which lit up the darkness were like a swarm of fireflies luring the weary to the town's bosom. It made the long ride worth while.

The two dishevelled riders had travelled 170 miles across vast prairies, forested mountains and even Indian territories to reach the remote town called Gun Fury. It had been a hard and hazardous trek and the strain of every mile of it showed on both riders and horses.

It had been at least eighty miles since they had last

seen a building, let alone a town. They eased back on their reins and rode side by side towards the welcome sight with the hope of a warm bath and shave in the minds of both of them.

Yet from a distance Gun Fury appeared far quieter than either of them had expected. Both men were in the autumn of their lives. Some less generous souls might even have said they had already ridden into their respective winters. At a time when most men were thinking of a rocking-chair or reserving a plot up on Boot Hill, this intrepid pair of riders simply rode on in a quest neither spoke of openly.

The West was getting itself fenced in and it was their ambition to find one day the freedom of their childhood. They hated the laws created by spineless people, which roped real men down for no good reason apart from fear. People who had never ridden beyond the Pecos river were slowly spreading their influence across what had once been a vast untamed and unnamed continent. No cancer could have been more threatening to those who had cherished those fast disappearing days.

Men in these lands wanted to be able to play keno, faro or poker and drink until they saw double. They wanted to be able to womanize, smoke and spit without folks fining them for not being polite.

They wanted to live hard, not simply exist waiting for the Grim Reaper.

Both horsemen knew that law was vital when it

21

gave the weak the power to punish the strong for killing or stealing. But when laws did nothing except make illegal everything menfolk did that was enjoyable, then it was time to ride on. When towns took root it was the barbers, whiskey drummers and whores who turned up first, closely followed by the merchants. They risked everything including their lives in those first few years, and then the Bible-punchers showed up. Only when it was safe, mind you. Then it was time to put civilization behind their horses' tails, spur hard and continue their search.

But this search was different from the previous ones they had undertaken. This time they were not looking for a place. This time they were seeking a legend.

A legend, it had been rumoured, that was in the town of Gun Fury.

The two riders would have crossed 1,000 miles of burning desert in order to reach the man who had saved both their lives a year or so back.

For ex-convict Tom Dix and retired lawman Dan Shaw sought a man named James Butler Hickok. Or Wild Bill as he had become known across the land. Like most legends in human form Hickok had his demons and they continued to haunt him. For demons can make even the stoutest of souls destroy themselves.

Men who are branded as legends find it hard to live up to others' expectations of what a legend ought to be. People crave heroes and create them whenever they get the chance. But men cannot ever live up to the myths created by those who admire them. For at the final sundown, they are just flesh and blood like the rest of mankind.

Hickok knew this better than most. He also knew it would be his own legend which would eventually destroy him.

Dix pointed at the wooden marker. He eased back and stopped his tall black stallion as his partner reined in beside him on his buckskin quarter horse.

Dan Shaw rubbed the trail grime from his features and beat the sweat from his hat against his chaps.

'What's it say, Dixie?' Dan asked.

Dix leaned over and struck a match with his thumbnail. Its flame lasted long enough for the rider to see the faded name of the town. He straightened up again.

'That's Gun Fury OK, Dan,' Dix sighed. 'We found it.'

'You sound a tad disappointed, pard,' Dan remarked. He replaced the hat upon his head.

Dix pushed his Stetson off his temple and allowed the sweat to trickle down his face. He tilted his head.

'I am,' he admitted. 'I was expecting the place to be a bit more noisy.'

'Why?' Dan pulled out a cigar and bit off its tip.

'If James Butler's there it oughta be a lot more fiery.'

Dan nodded slowly and accepted a match from his pal. He ran it across his saddle horn and cupped the flame. He sucked in the smoke and inhaled deeply.

'Yeah! Now you mention it, Gun Fury don't look very lively.'

'I seen ghost towns look more alive than that place.' Dix smiled and stared at the vast range around them. The snowcapped mountains were far behind them now but he still recalled the cold that had chewed into the very marrow of his bones a week or so earlier. 'Think on it, Dan. Why would James Butler be holding up there?'

Dan blew smoke out.

'You know Wild Bill, Dixie. He goes on a drunk every now and then. Sometimes it kinda lasts a little bit longer than is good for a man. But that's where we got the wire from.'

Dix looked at the swaying telegraph poles that stretched towards the horizon. The starlight danced along their wires.

'That's another thing that's been gnawing at my craw, Dan.' Dix said thoughtfully. 'How come he sent us a telegraph message to meet him here? And how'd he know we was in Waco in the first place?'

Dan rolled the smoke around in his mouth before blowing it at the neck of his buckskin. 'You fret too much, Dixie. You always gotta ask dumb questions. Bill must have heard someone speak of us in a saloon or the like.'

'Maybe.' Dix snorted. 'But it don't figure none. I got me a feeling that we've been lured into a trap.'

'By who?'

Dix waved his left hand aimlessly. 'We got us enemies, Dan. It could be someone with a grudge. We've killed a few bad apples in our time and most of them got kinfolk.'

'Think of the hot soapy water and the chance for us to get out of this stinking trail gear and put some clean clothes on, Dixie,' Dan smiled.

Dix nodded and stared at the streetlights flickering in the town. There were far fewer than he would have expected in a town the size of Gun Fury. He turned his eyes back to his friend.

'You got the time?'

Dan pulled out his half hunter and held the golden timepiece close to the glowing tip of his cigar. It gave just enough illumination for him to see the hands of the golden pocket watch.

'It ain't even seven yet, Dixie,' Dan said in surprise. 'I thought it was a whole lot later than that.'

'Maybe Gun Fury takes longer than most towns to wake up and get going, Dan.' The leaner man of the pair shrugged and tapped his spurs gently. The stallion began to walk on with the buckskin mount at its side.

The horses followed the well-worn route carved out by countless herds of steers over the years. They headed towards the remote settlement at an even pace. The smoke trailed from Dan Shaw's mouth as he kept staring at the wooden buildings ahead of them.

'You reckon they got a bathtub in this town, Dixie?' he asked. 'I'm powerful in need of a good soaking.'

Dix did not reply. His thoughts were on the man they had been looking for. He knew, more than most, of the problems the famed Hickok suffered from. The closer they got to the long main street the more he started to wonder whether Hickok had chosen this remote place for another reason. They rode over the railtracks and could clearly see the numerous wooden markers bathed in starlight on a ridge overlooking the town. Every town had its own Boot Hill. This town's Boot Hill just seemed a lot bigger than most, Dix thought.

'What you thinking about, Dixie?' Dan asked as they rode side by side.

'I got me a feeling Gun Fury looks like the kinda place Bill would choose to die in, Dan,' Dix answered bluntly. 'You know he has always reckoned that some coward would backshoot him one day just to get himself a reputation.'

Dan inhaled deeply and savoured the smoke. He had a feeling his partner was right.

'Can't be easy being as famous as he is,' Dan reasoned. 'There's always someone ready to try and steal your glory!'

'That's why our James Butler always sits with his back to the nearest wall,' Dix said.

'I'd hate to be feared like that.'

Suddenly as they reached the outskirts of the town a shot rang out. Its sound echoed around the wooden buildings and made the horses tied to hitching rails along Main Street drag at their tethers.

Dix stood in his stirrups and whipped the shoulders of his stallion. The powerful animal charged towards the heart of the town. Dix looked back.

'C'mon, Dan. Let's find out where that shooting come from.'

Dan spurred. 'Damn it all! Wait for me, Dixie!'

THREE

The horses tethered at hitching rails shied as the sturdy pair of mounts thundered down the wide street in search of the place from where the gunshot had sounded. Dix pulled back on his reins and stopped his powerful mount just yards from the two lawmen who had only seconds earlier stepped down on to the sandy street. Dan managed to haul his quarter horse to a standstill a few feet behind his partner.

The first man was burly. At least fifty with a gleaming star pinned to his vest. The second man was far younger, thin and less secure behind his own tin star. Both held on to their double-barrelled scatterguns with similar muscular hands though.

Marshal Elroy Cooper looked as though he, like the pair of riders who faced him, was from another time. A waxed handlebar moustache was well-trimmed and spanned the entire width of his face from ear to ear. His small eyes stared out from beneath the brim of his black Stetson at the strangers who were steadying their horses. Cooper turned the barrels of his hefty weapon on to the nearesr horseman and pulled back the gun's hammers.

The sound of them locking filled the street.

'Was it you that fired that shot?' Cooper asked Dix before turning his eyes to Dan. 'Or was it you?'

Dix dismounted and looped his reins across the nearest hitching rail. He secured them firmly, then looked into the marshal's face.

'Neither of us, Marshal,' he drawled.

'We just rode in and was looking to see if we could find who did send that shot off,' Dan added as he eased his aching frame off the buckskin.

The deputy edged closer to the marshal's shoulder. He whispered in Cooper's ear.

'I don't like the looks of these varmints, Marshal.'

Cooper glanced at Bobby Sanders and nodded firmly. 'Me neither, Bobby! I've seen me a lotta bad'uns in my time and they all looked like this pair. Mean and ugly!'

'Who you calling ugly?' Dix asked.

Dan Shaw tied up his horse next to his pal's, then walked up to the lawmen.

'The name's Shaw,' he said touching the brim of his hat. 'Dan Shaw. Retired US marshal.'

Cooper looked at Sanders and then back at the

man who was caked in trail dust.

'I reckon you can prove that, old-timer?'

Dan patted his coat pockets until he located his wallet. He pulled it free and handed it to the man who still had his scattergun aimed at Dix. Cooper studied the papers and nodded to himself.

'Papers can be forged,' Cooper muttered as he returned the wallet to its owner.

'Mine ain't!'

Sanders aimed a thin finger at Dix. 'Who is he? He sure don't look like no lawman I ever set eyes on!'

'You could be right, Bobby. He ain't never bin a lawman,' the marshal stated. 'I'd bet my hat on that!'

Dan nodded. 'That's my pal Tom Dix, Marshal.'

Cooper's eyes widened slightly. 'The gunfighter?'

Dan nodded. 'One and the same.'

'I thought Dix was locked up!' Cooper exclaimed.

'I served my time, Marshal,' Dix said.

Elroy Cooper lowered his gun and stepped even closer to Dan Shaw. He looked puzzled.

'What's a retired lawman doing riding with an ex-convict, old-timer? Ain't you got any pride?'

'Dixie saved my life and served twelve years for being honest enough to admit he made a mistake, Marshal,' Dan explained. 'He could have hightailed it and never have served a single day in prison but he faced the music and it cost him dear. Tom Dix is the finest man I ever met.'

30

Cooper put the scattergun under his left arm and held out his hand to Dan.

'The name's Cooper, Mr Shaw.'

Dan shook the hand. 'They call me Dan, Cooper.'

The marshal looked at Dix. He held out his hand to the thin figure and smiled.

'When a law officer says that someone is the finest man they ever met, it's gotta be true!'

Dix accepted the handshake. 'They call me Dixie, Marshal.'

'You trust this pair, Marshal?' the deputy asked.

'Oh, hush up, Bobby,' Cooper said. 'I'm glad to have me some professional help for once, boy.'

'I'm a professional lawman,' Sanders sniffed.

'I know, but your ma is my sister,' Cooper said. 'It ain't the same as meeting another man who has worn a marshal's star, Bobby.'

The deputy rested his scattergun on his shoulder and looked offended. 'I'm telling Ma about what you said, Uncle Elroy. You see if I don't tell.'

Dix glanced at Dan, then they both stared down at the ground.

Suddenly their laughter was cut short. Another shot rang out. The entire length of Main Street seemed to come to life as men and bargirls walked out from the various saloons and stared up and down the thoroughfare.

The deputy raised his scattergun and looked down towards the distant livery-stable building.

31

'I figure it came from down thataway,' Sanders announced.

Dix drew one of his Colts, cocked its hammer and pointed its barrel at an alleyway between the bank and the marshal's office.

'I figure it came from down there.'

Dan nodded and pulled his own gun.

Both men ran.

Marshal Cooper slapped the deputy across the ear. 'C'mon, you lame brain! If we listened to you we'd be chasing echoes!'

Reluctantly the young man followed his three elders between the two buildings.

The alley was dark.

No streetlights reached this place. It was somewhere that only shadows ever found. Dix moved like a man half his actual age and managed to negotiate the twists and turns between the high wooden-walled alleyway. He avoided the trash barrels until his legs took him to a wide-open area backed on to by four buildings. He stopped and looked all around him. The lights from two windows cascaded down into the empty area but it was still darker than Dix liked. Across the open area another two alleys led away.

The others caught up with the gunfighter and stopped beside him. Dix turned to the marshal.

'What is this place for?' Dix asked.

'It ain't *for* nothing,' Sanders answered before the

marshal could open his mouth. 'It just happened when the dudes who built the houses finished.'

'Young'uns used to play in here,' Cooper added.

'They don't any more?' Dan queried.

The marshal looked at Dan. 'There ain't more than half a dozen kids in town nowadays. Most folks moved on when the railroad quit coming to Gun Fury.'

Dix waved his left hand at his three companions in a gesture that told them to stop talking. They obeyed as the thin man walked across into the centre of the yard.

With every step Dix turned his head and studied the wooden walls. His gun barrel remained cocked and ready as he ventured further and further away from the three other men. His ears listened hard for what his eyes could not see. There was something wrong here. Every sinew of his body told him so. He had learned long ago never to question or ignore his gut feelings.

Bobby Sanders leaned closer to the marshal and whispered:

'What's that old fool looking for, Marshal?'

Cooper gave a sigh and slapped his deputy around the ear again. The deputy winced.

'Hush up, Bobby! Look and you might just learn something!'

Dan eased forward a few steps, then stopped again. He too was looking all around the eerily quiet yard. He had learned long ago never to question his partner when it came to such things as this. Dix was like a bloodhound. He could locate a smoking gun barrel blindfolded.

Dix reached the wooden wall opposite and rested a shoulder against it. He stared up into the black alley and bit his lip thoughtfully.

Suddenly his memory returned to a time nearly twenty years earlier when he had chased a gunman through the back streets and alleyways of another town. He had made a big mistake then, had squeezed the trigger and killed the wrong man.

It had cost him twelve years of his life.

Dix did not want to repeat his deadly mistake.

Dan quietly walked to his side. 'What you reckon is up there, Dixie?'

Dix pointed at his own nose and sniffed the night air. Dan copied the action and then realized what his partner meant. The aroma of gunpowder still hung around the mouth of the alley. Dix had been correct. This had to be the place where the gun had been fired.

But who had fired that shot and why?

The questions nagged at Dix.

The marshal and his deputy crossed the expanse of sand and reached the two men beside the entrance to the alley. They too were cautious about entering a place where blackness ruled.

'What you stopped for?' The deputy asked with a

shaking voice. 'I thought you was a gunfighter, Mr Dix? You ain't scared of the dark, are you?'

'Hush up, Bobby!' the marshal ordered. 'Dix is a gunfighter but he ain't loco!'

Dix turned and looked at the lawmen.

'You got anything that we could use to cast a little light into this alley? A bunch of rags or the like? Maybe a kerosene lantern. Anything to light up that alley.'

Suddenly, before either Cooper or Sanders could reply, a shaft of red-hot light cut out from the alley. Then its sound deafened their ears.

'That critter is still up there,' Cooper gasped.

'It's a good thing we didn't go strolling in, Dixie,' Dan added.

'I thought he was still up there! I could smell his gun!' Dix pushed himself up against the wooden wall and looked carefully around the corner down into the alley. He screwed up his eyes and vainly tried to see the gunman. Then another taper of venom blasted at him. This time Dix's Stetson was torn from his head before the sound of the bullet reached them. Dix reeled on the heels of his boots and fell to his knees. The gloved fingers of his left hand clasped his forehead. Soon blood dripped from between them.

Dan dropped down beside his pal.

'Let me look, Dixie,' he said. He forced the fingers away from the gash that had parted his partner's hair.

'We better find a doctor, Dixie. You need sewing up.'

'That dirty bushwhacker!' Dix forced himself back up to his full height and pushed his concerned partner aside. He raised his Colt and squeezed its trigger. His shot lit up the dark alley enough for him to see a figure turn and run.

The gunfighter fanned the hammer of his gun another five times. Each of his bullets lit up the alley as flame spewed from the barrel of his .45.

Dan grabbed his friend and pulled him to the cover of the wooden wall.

'Dixie!' he shouted repeatedly until Dix shook the anger from his eyes.

'He's gone, Dan,' Dix muttered. 'I could see the jasper running away in the light of my gunfire.'

'The yella bastard!' Dan snorted.

'I seen something else, Dan,' Dix said.

'Yeah?' Dan asked.

Dix nodded.

'Yeah, pard.'

The deputy had climbed up the wooden wall and plucked a rusty lantern from its lofty perch atop a high pole. He returned to the three others and shook it beside his right ear. A broad grin crossed his face.

'There's enough oil in here to light up all of creation, I reckon,' Sanders said excitedly.

Dix handed a match to the young man. 'Light it, boy! We're gonna take us a look down this alleyway.'

'What you figure we'll find, Dix?' Cooper asked.

'What was it you saw, Dixie?' Dan wondered aloud.

Dix rubbed the blood from his face, wiped it on his pants leg and then swiftly exchanged his guns. He cocked the hammer of the new one until it fully locked.

'A dead'un, boys,' he replied. 'I saw me a dead'un!'

FOUR

There was a storm brewing at the Golden Spur. Every man inside the plush surroundings of the saloon watched the tall figure seated at the poker table. Hickok drew attention even though he was obviously the worse for wear. He had played poker for nearly thirty minutes and yet seemed unable to find a winning hand. Once he had been able to bluff his way to winning most pots but that gift had eluded him since arriving in Gun Fury. The dwindling stack of chips told the story not one of the other players or onlookers dared to utter. He reached across to his left, lifted the bottle of whiskey and filled his glass again.

'You calling, Wild Bill?' the player opposite him asked as he held his own five cards to his chest. The other four players also waited.

Hickok placed his cards down and shook his head.

'I fold.' He heaved a sighed.

The player smiled. All of the other players smiled. Every man in the long bar room smiled. Once again one of them had bettered the famous Hickok. The man who had once earned most of his living from his ability with a deck of fifty-two was now on the ropes and losing heavily. It was like being a witness to a prize fighter who had taken on one opponent too many. When legends fall they fall further than mere mortals. They fall from the pedestals upon which others have placed them.

'Reckon I win,' the man said, throwing his own cards face up on to the green baize. The other gamblers all nodded in agreement and tossed their cards into the middle of the table.

Hickok downed his whiskey and used his index finger to flick the cards at the pile of multicoloured chips.

'Maybe you ought to quit for tonight, Wild Bill?' another of the players suggested.

The head turned and the hooded eyes looked hard at the man who had dared to speak. Hickok poured another glass of the amber liquor into his glass and stared at it.

'You talking to me, sonny?' Hickok muttered angrily.

The man looked nervous. 'I just thought you look a tad tired tonight, Wild Bill!'

'I've killed a lot of men in my time for talking to me like that, boy!' The hooded eyes narrowed. They returned to the player and burned into him. 'Maybe I ought to pistol whip you until you learn a little respect!'

The man waved his hands before him fearfully.

'There ain't no call for you beating on me, Wild Bill.'

'I'll decide that, boy.'

Rufas Hardy was behind the long bar counter and could hear every word as the room went into a hush. It was as if every man in the saloon was waiting for the famed gunfighter with the long hair to show he was still a force to be reckoned with. There was the smell of excitement in the stale, smoke-filled air. No cock fight could have drawn more anticipation. Hardy leaped over the counter and started towards the table.

'I'm gonna shoot your damn knees off!' Hickok pushed his chair back until it touched the wall and then went to stand. Yet the long legs no longer obeyed as once they had done. He clumsily faltered and fell to the floor. For a moment he just lay on the floor and stared with blurred eyes at the shoes and boots that surrounded him.

Then he heard the mocking comments coming from all around the busy room. The barely muffled laughter. He went to rise and grabbed out at the table leg. His hand found the spittoon instead. It fell over and its contents spread over him.

Then he felt the arms around him.

40

It was Rufas and another man. They hauled the tall gunfighter off the floor and walked him towards the drapes.

'You need sleep, Wild Bill. Not gunplay.'

'Hold up,' Hickok slurred. 'I ain't finished drinking yet!'

'But, Bill,' Rufas Hardy whispered, 'you're ill.'

'Take me there!' Hickok aimed a bony finger at the seat close to the wall near the entrance where he had spent most of the day. 'And bring me my damn bottle!'

The owner of the saloon and his companion obeyed. They eased Hickok into the chair behind the round drinking table. They watched as the man leaned back until his mane of long hair touched the wallpaper.

'Get his bottle and glass, Johnny,' Rufas said as he made sure that his best guest was not going to fall to the floor again and add even more humiliation to his sorry state.

Hickok blinked hard. It did not clear the fog from his eyes. All he could see were colours and shapes. But he could hear the laughter and the words though.

'Look at the great Wild Bill Hickok, boys,' someone said loudly. 'Propped up against the wall with other folks' spittle all over him.'

'It's a shame,' another voice said.

'Now he's just another old drunk.'

41

Hickok felt the hand on his face as fingers pushed his long hair from his sweat-soaked skin.

'My bottle!' Hickok snarled drunkenly.

'Here it is, Bill,' Rufas said as his friend handed the bottle and glass to him. 'Take it easy.'

'Don't they know who I am, Rufas?' Hickok muttered as he swayed on the chair.

'They know OK, Bill.' Rufas patted the shoulder of the man who had not washed either himself or his clothes for weeks and who now stank. 'Trouble is they ain't afraid.'

Hickok rested his hands on his gun grips. 'They ought to be afraid, Rufas.'

Rufas leaned close and whispered. 'Only you can make them afraid, Bill. But not like this. You have to stop drinking for a while so your mind clears.'

'It ain't my mind I want clearing, Rufas.' Hickok lifted the glass and downed its contents.

'You're killing yourself, Bill.'

'Maybe it's better that I do it before some wet nosed young bastard does it for me.'

'You're Wild Bill Hickok,' Rufas told the man with half-closed eyes. 'None of them can ever be that.'

'But why ain't they afraid any more?' Hickok slurred. 'They ought to be afraid. Why ain't they afraid?'

'You ain't gonna find the answer in the bottom of a whiskey bottle, Bill.'

'I can try, Rufas. I can damn well try!'

Tom Dix had pulled his bandanna from around his neck and held it against the bleeding graze. But blood still traced its way down his rugged features. He and Dan watched the nervous deputy holding the lantern above the crumpled corpse as Cooper knelt down and turned the body over. The marshal gasped and looked up at his trio of companions.

'This is Brad Smithers,' he announced.

'Who might that be, Cooper?' Dan asked curiously.

'The bank teller,' the law officer replied.

Dan looked at Dix. 'I got me a feeling that this might not be a random murder, Dixie. Not when there's a bank involved.'

'Did he have keys to the bank?' Dix asked.

Cooper shrugged. 'Now that's something I don't know. We'll have to find out from Jed Smith, the bank manager.'

The injured gunfighter said nothing. He just nodded and turned away from the gruesome sight. He walked along the alley until he reached the corner, then stopped.

'Hey, Bobby,' Dix said, 'bring that lantern here.'

Both lawmen left the blood-soaked sand and trailed Dan until they all reached Dix's side.

'What's the matter, Dixie?' Dan questioned his pal.

Dix took the lantern from the deputy and raised it

until its light flowed over the wooden wall. A close group of bullets was embedded in the wall.

'Mighty fine shooting, Dixie,' Cooper said approvingly.

Dix glanced through his own blood at Dan. 'What do you see, Dan?'

'Bullet holes, pard,' Dan said, shrugging. 'What else?'

'*Five* bullet holes, Dan,' Dix pointed out.

All three men leaned closer to the wooden wall and counted the holes. They remained silent.

'I emptied my gun at that critter, boys!' Dix said. 'Yet only five of my slugs are here!'

Sanders snapped his young fingers. 'I know what you must be getting at, Dixie.'

Cooper looked at his deputy. 'You do?'

'Sure enough.' Sanders nodded firmly and pointed at the planks. 'There ain't no way that a man with the gun skills of Dixie could miss a solid wall. So if there's only five bullets here that means one of 'em hit something else!'

Dan smiled and turned to his pal.

'You winged the killer, Dixie.'

Dix lowered the lantern until it was a few inches above the sandy ground. He stared for a few moments and then saw what he was looking for.

'See them blood drops?'

Dan knelt down and then aimed a finger in the direction of a back street. 'They ain't yours, Dixie.

They lead off down thataway!'

'We oughta follow them blood drops,' Sanders said.

'Nope!' Dix muttered after he straightened up. 'They won't lead us to the killer if he's half as smart as I reckon he is.'

The marshal nodded in agreement. 'Dix is right. That jasper might lead us round in circles all night until he manages to stem the flow of his wound. If he has himself a horse around here someplace there ain't no way we'll be able to trail him.'

Dix returned his attention back to the body and began to walk back towards it.

The others followed.

'You got an undertaker in this town, Cooper?'

Marshal Cooper rubbed his chin. 'Not a real one any more. The last year or so we bin getting Luke Stone up in the livery to bury our dead.'

'He's real good at it,' the deputy added. 'He'll bury anyone for a bottle of good red eye.'

'By the look of all them markers up on Boot Hill your Luke has bin mighty busy,' Dan said.

Dix gave the lantern to Dan and then looked at the marshal. 'Is there a doc in Gun Fury, Cooper?'

Again the marshal had to shrug.

'I'm afraid not, Dixie. Joe Benson the barber is mighty good at mending bones and stitching folks up, though. He'll even dig out the odd lump of lead if'n he gets paid.'

Dix let out a sigh. 'Looks like I'm going to the barber shop to get myself sewn up.'

Cooper waved Sanders to the opposite end of the bank teller's remains. Both men reached down and got hold of the limp body.

Dix watched as the lawman lifted the body up off the sand and started to carry it back towards the yard. He looked at Dan, then started to follow.

'I didn't have the heart to ask if there's anywhere we can get a bath, Dan.'

Dan shook his head solemnly. 'Our luck's running kinda thin, ain't it?'

'Yep,' Dix replied. 'Well, mine is anyways.'

FIVE

Like the surgeons of old, Joe Benson the barber expertly snipped the end of the catgut at the crown of Dix's bloodied scalp and stepped back to admire his handiwork. He was satisfied and it showed. Dix stared into the smoke-stained mirror and then at the reflections of Cooper and Dan who sat behind him. His head still felt as though a stick of dynamite had exploded inside his skull but at least the bleeding had stopped.

'Good job, Joe,' Dix said.

'Thank you kindly, Mr Dix.'

'You look a mess, Dixie,' Dan offered.

'Back to normal then,' Dix said. He eased himself from the black leather-and-steel chair and leaned against it. He was tired and had lost a lot of blood. 'Did you get our bedrolls off the horses with our fresh gear, Dan?'

'Sure enough!' Dan patted the bedrolls on a vacant hardback chair next to him.

'You boys want a bath?' Joe Benson asked. 'My barbershop might not be the best there is but we got us a damn tidy bath house out back and the water's always hot.'

Eagerly Dan rose from his chair faster than a man of his age ought to be able to move and grabbed the barber's arm.

'Show me.'

The barber chuckled and turned to face the drape which led to the bathhouse at the rear of his shop. He paused and touched the gunfighter's arm.

'Are you OK, Mr Dix?'

Dix forced a smile. 'Thanks, Joe! You stopped me losing the last few drops of my blood in true fashion, I'm grateful. At my age I can't afford to lose too much!'

The barber nodded. 'Shall I run a bath for you as well?'

Dix returned the nod. 'That would be good. Much obliged.'

Marshal Cooper pointed at the barber's chair.

'You should sit back down, Dixie, before you pass out. I ain't seen nothing quite as white as you are.'

Dix did as advised and returned his thin frame to the well-padded barber's chair. He gave a long sigh, then leaned forward to study the brutal wound on his scalp in the mirror.

'I reckon I'd better start combing my hair the other way from now on, Cooper,' he said.

'That might not be so easy.' Cooper smiled through cigar smoke. The lawman dragged himself up from the chair and closed the distance between them. He rested a hand on the brass rail which ran across the length of the window. His eyes ignored his own reflection and stared out into the dimly lit street. A few horsemen rode past. He then eased himself around and faced the injured Dix again.

'You never told me why you and Dan are in Gun Fury, Dixie,' he drawled. 'This ain't a town that's on the way to any place. Folks who come here nowadays are mostly outlaws looking for a place to hide away from the authorities. You boys lost?'

Dix used his boots to move the chair around until he was facing the stout lawman.

'Me and Dan had us a telegraph wire from an old pal.'

'Who might that be?'

'Hickok' Dix said the name and watched the marshal's face for his reaction. It was always the same whenever he said the name to anyone. It was a name which created a picture in the minds of everyone. 'Is he in town?'

'Wild Bill Hickok sure is in town, Dixie,' Cooper said. He put the cigar back between his teeth. 'He's a pal of yours, huh?'

Dix nodded.

'Yep. So he's in Gun Fury, Cooper. I had started to think that someone had led us down here on a fools errand.'

'He sure is and I'll not say that I'm happy about it, Dixie.'

'Why not?' Dix was surprised.

'Men like Hickok draw vermin, Dixie.' Cooper sighed through a cloud of smoke. 'Men like him are magnets to vermin hell-bent on making a reputation for themselves. He's bin here for a month or so and I've already seen a score or more gunslingers turn up for no good reason.'

'They got a reason,' Dix muttered.

'Yep. Like I said, vermin hoping to make a name for themselves as being the one who finishes off the famous Wild Bill Hickok. Could make them famous and even rich.'

'Or just dead!' Dix argued.

'He's no match for anyone at the moment, Dixie,' Cooper said with a hint of sadness in his tone. 'He's on a drunk and the only thing keeping him alive is his reputation, but that can't last for ever. I can't believe that he's the same guy I used to read all them stories about.'

'Sometimes it ain't easy being famous,' Dix said. 'It eats at a man's soul.'

'I've heard about you and how good you are with them guns but I don't see you diving into no whiskey bottle, Dixie,' Cooper observed.

'Nobody ever wrote no tall stories about me, Cooper.'

Cooper looked straight at Dix. 'If'n he don't sober up, he's gonna end up dead pretty soon. If you're his pal then get him out of Gun Fury.'

Dix ran a thumbnail along his unshaven jaw. He knew what the marshal meant.

'Has he killed anyone yet?'

'Not yet but he will.' Cooper paced around the shop and stared down at the hair at his feet.

'Me and Dan have known him for nearly half our lives,' Dix said. 'I know that he can have his moments and skim the law damn close. But at heart he's a good man.'

'He's a damn drunk, Dixie!' Cooper snapped. 'He ain't quit drinking since he hit town and that's dangerous. Drunks with a pair of hoglegs like he's carrying are dangerous.'

Suddenly Tom Dix noticed something. Someone was missing from the small group of men who had chased the killer into the dark alleys.

'Where's your deputy?' Dix asked as he suddenly realized that it was the youngster who was not with them any longer.

'I sent him to tell old Smith that his teller is dead,' came the reply from the marshal. 'I also told him to ask if Brad had keys to the bank on him.'

Dix nodded. 'If you need help me and Dan volunteer.'

51

Cooper rested a hand on the back of the barber chair. He gazed at the gunfighter's stitched scalp and then up at the mirror. Dix's eyes were trained on his every movement. The lawman leaned close to Dix's right ear.

'You ever seen Wild Bill in action?'

'Yep,' Dix replied.

'Is he as good with them guns of his as all them stories say he is, Dixie?'

'Better.'

Cooper tapped the ash from his cigar, walked to the door and turned its handle. He paused and looked back at the man in the chair.

'He's staying at the Golden Spur, Dixie. You want that I rent you boys a room when I'm on my rounds?'

Dix raised a hand and touched his temple. 'Thanks, *amigo*.' The marshal opened the door, stepped out on to the boardwalk and closed the door behind him. Dix watched as his sturdy figure walked out across the street towards his office.

The barber returned to his shop and rubbed his hands together.

'Your pard is up to his neck in soapsuds, Mr Dix. And I've got a tub waiting for you as well.'

Dix touched his chin. 'I'll have me a shave first, Joe.'

'You'll feel like a new man when I'm finished with you.' The barber picked up his straight razor and checked its honed edge.

'I sure hope so,' Dix said. 'This old one is real beat up and kinda worn out at the moment!'

SIX

Bobby Sanders had done everything his uncle had commanded him to do and was headed back to the marshal's office with his hefty weapon balanced on his shoulder. He had awoken the banker from his early night's slumber and discovered that Brad Smithers, the teller, did not have any keys to the bank. He would inform Cooper when he reached the office and the coffee pot which was never allowed to stop brewing atop the wood-burning stove.

More than half of Gun Fury had become strangely eerie since the majority of the population had abandoned their homes and businesses. The streets had once been a lot brighter than they were now, when every store along the main street had been occupied. Then every lamp on the high poles was lit and every building's windows and opened doors allowed illumination to flood out into the street.

Now the only lights were those that shone from

the saloons and the few businesses that remained.

Shadows now dominated Gun Fury. And where there were shadows there was usually vermin of all shapes and sizes. Both four-legged and two-legged creatures lurked where the light did not penetrate, to prey on the filth and sorrow of others.

Sanders stepped off one walkway and was headed across a sandy side street towards the boardwalk that led past the adjacent Longhorn and Broken Bottle saloons.

The side street was shrouded in blackness. Not a place to venture into without protection.

For some reason the deputy paused and looked along it. He could make out the roofs of a few of the houses and boarded-up stores in the starlight but nothing else was visible. It was as though someone had painted everything with the blackest of paints.

The sight chilled the deputy.

The sound of boots on wooden planks caught his attention. He screwed up his young eyes and vainly attempted to see who it was walking in the shadows.

Then the boots went silent.

Whoever it was had stopped.

He heard the sound of a door open and then close. Bobby Sanders shrugged and rammed both hands into his pants pocket. He walked swiftly to the boardwalk, mounted the three steps and then continued along. The smell of hard liquor filled his nostrils from both saloons as their lights flooded over and under their swing doors.

Being of a curious turn of mind the tall youngster slowed and glanced into the interiors of both saloons in hope of seeing the few females who plied their trade to the town's menfolk. It was forbidden fruit but he sure had an appetite growing inside his young loins. An appetite that he knew would one day be satisfied.

He gave a chuckle and then moved on towards the marshal's office set close to the bank.

Not all vermin was afraid to show itself. Philo Chance was the eldest of three brothers and son to one of the few remaining ranchers who still grazed their herds on the range outside Gun Fury. Pop Chance was a man somewhere in his sixties and one of the most crooked of his breed, but even he could not hold a candle to the actions of his first-born.

For Philo had a madness in him that had never been understood or fully contained. It was a sickness that showed itself in his often bizarre behaviour. In his twenty-eight years of life he had never been out of trouble and had killed countless people for the most trivial of reasons.

Yet the Chances were a fearful clan with more than a dozen hired cowboys to protect them from the law's ever bringing any of them to book.

Philo Chance had always managed to remain a free man because no lawman had ever had the guts to tackle the entire family. And when faced with the Chances no lawman had ever managed to raise a posse willing to go up against them.

The depraved Philo Chance had begun to think he could do anything without fear of retribution and the notches on his pair of six-guns proved his point.

The brooding cattleman had been on a drunk for nearly two days and nights. He staggered along the dark side street towards the main thoroughfare, avoiding all the lights as the people in Gun Fury always tried to avoid him. With guns hung low Philo Chance had the reputation of being so mad that there was nothing and no one he would not turn his Colts on and kill.

He rested a shoulder on an porch upright, pushed a cigarette between his lips and stared down into Main Street.

Gunsmoke still rose from the barrel of one of his guns as it sat in the holster on his left thigh. As he struck a match and sucked in smoke his thoughts returned to an hour earlier when he had bumped into Brad Smithers.

Smithers had been a mild-mannered soul who had never swerved from the straight and narrow.

The cowboy laughed to himself.

He had enjoyed killing the bank teller but had been annoyed when he could not find any keys to the bank on the man. For Philo had run low on cash and wanted to keep drinking. He had thought he would be able to unlock the bank's rear door and just stroll in to help himself to any money that had not been put in the safe.

Philo Chance kicked at the dust and inhaled even more deeply on his twisted smoke.

There was no feeling of remorse for killing the meek bank teller. Not a scrap of guilt within the degenerate creature's heart.

Just anger that his plan had gone sour.

He rubbed his unshaven face with filthy blood-covered hands and narrowed his eyes. He could see a man walking hastily long the end of the street. A man who was buttoning up his coat and continually adjusting his brown derby hat.

Philo swung on the upright and leaned away from the porch overhang. With the smoking cigarette between his lips he continued to watch the man in a way a puma watches potential prey.

The figure was well-dressed and looked as though he might have more than a few dollars in his pockets. Dollars which would allow the eldest of the Chance brothers to resume his drinking.

The man was moving quickly.

Too quickly, Chance told himself.

Soon he would be away from the darkest end of the long street and into the light of the saloons.

Philo knew he would have to act fast if he were to rob this man and get away without anyone seeing him. He released his grip on the upright, then he felt

the numb pain in his right shoulder. He paused and
turned his head. The top of his jacket shoulder had
been hit by a bullet. Blood covered the right-hand
side of his coat. He raised a hand and touched the
shoulder but there was no pain. Only blood.

Chance peeled the ripped fabric away and saw that
he had been nicked by the bullet of the man he had
tried to kill back in the dark alley. The man who had
interrupted him when he had shot the bank teller.

He blinked hard and returned his eyes to the man
who was getting closer as his short, fat legs carried
him on. Suddenly Philo Chance realized he knew
who the man was.

'Smith!' Chance muttered quietly.

Jed Smith had more than just a few dollars to his
name. The banker must be the richest person in Gun
Fury, Chance told himself.

This was a prize worth going for.

He dropped his left hand, pulled his smoking .45
from its holster and stepped down into the street. He
moved towards the man in a fashion he often used
when atop a cutting horse trying to stop a maverick
from escaping his rope.

This was the banker and he had to have on him
the keys to the bank, even the safe in which most of
the money would be kept. For it was well known that
Smith trusted no one. He had to have his keys upon
him, Philo thought.

Chance moved fast for a man who had managed to

consume more than three bottles of whiskey since arriving in Gun Fury. He reached the darker end of the street long before the banker found the protective light of coal-tar lanterns.

Like the experinced cowpuncher he was, Chance stopped Jed Smith in his tracks. He pushed the barrel of his six-shooter into the belly of the banker.

'What are you doing, Philo?' the outraged Smith boomed.

'Shut the hell up and git into them shadows!' Chance snarled.

The banker walked backwards as the barrel of the weapon pushed into him. He could see the lights getting further away from him as the lane came closer.

'Stop this foolishness, Philo!' Smith implored.

With no warning, Chance raised the gun and whipped it savagely across the man's face. He smiled as the rotund figure fell over the boardwalk and landed at the entry to the lane. The cowboy leapt over the boards and landed next to his stunned victim. He cocked the gun's hammer and pushed it into the bleeding cheek of the dazed Smith.

'This is madness, Philo!' Smith groaned.

'I already killed Brad tonight, old man. I'm in the mood for more blood spilling,' Chance bragged.

Smith's eyes widened in horror. 'You're plumb loco!'

'Loco, huh?' Chance tore at the man's clothing

until he located the elusive metal ring that held the large keys to the bank. 'Git up! We're gonna strip that bank clean of every damn cent inside it.'

Smith felt himself being dragged back to his feet. His head was spinning and half his teeth were busted. Blood was running from his mouth and his cheek. The cowboy pushed the gun into the banker's back.

'Walk or die, Jed.'

Smith walked.

SEVEN

It was nearly ten when Dix and Dan led their mounts through the dimly lit street towards the Golden Spur. Thanks to the barber's best efforts they both smelled real sweet as they reached the first of the hitching poles and secured their reins. Dan rubbed his new pants.

'I hates new clothes,' he complained. 'I reckon there's half a ton of starch in each pants leg. Cutting me up more than that old quarter horse of mine done.'

Dix rested his hip against the hitching rail and studied the other few horses tethered along the front of the saloon. Then from the shadows a soft feminine voice spoke.

'Howdy, strangers.'

Both Dix and his pard turned and squinted into the darkness beneath the porch overhang. Then they saw a red glow about five feet from the weathered boards. Whoever the female was, she was smoking, Dix thought to himself.

Dan removed his hat and stooped under the pole and made his way to Dix's side.

'Howdy, ma'am,' Dan answered.

She moved forward into the glow of the streetlights. Her perfume overwhelmed everything Joe the barber had soaked them in and filled both men's nostrils. She appeared to be pretty but both men knew it was unwise to rely upon mere eyesight when studying a woman of the night. She probably had a quarter-inch of powder and paint covering her face.

'You keeping that hat on?' she asked Dix as her small, buttoned shoes reached the very edge of the boardwalk and stopped. 'Ain't you got manners like your pal?'

'My head is kinda messed up under this new hat, ma'am,' Dix said, his eyes travelling up and down the overdressed female.

Dan leaned towards her, clutching his hat against his belly.

'Dixie is telling the truth. Somebody shot his old hat off and took a chunk of his scalp with it.'

She appeared untroubled.

'Shame!'

'My name's Dan Shaw and this is Dixie, ma'am.'

'They call me Molly.' She sucked on her cigarette

with blood-red lips and then fluttered her eyelashes at both men. 'Molly Doyle.'

'Pleasure to meet you, ma'am.' Dan nodded as Dix stepped up on to the boardwalk and paused beside the female. He was at least a foot taller than she. He looked at her face long and hard.

'Seen anything you like, Dixie?'

'Yep.' Dix smiled and touched the brim of his hat with a finger. 'But I'm a tad too busy at the moment to gossip.'

Dan stepped up beside her and he also looked hard at her face. 'You are real pretty, Molly.'

'Much obliged, Dan.' She tossed the remnant of her smoke at the sand and then touched the back of her pinned-up hair in a way all females do when they think they might have a fish on the end of their line. 'You ain't so bad-looking yourself for an old-timer.'

Dix placed a hand on his pal's shoulder. 'C'mon! We can talk to Molly later, Dan. We got things to do first.'

'We have?'

'We gotta check out Wild Bill and then get our horses up to the livery.'

'Oh yeah!' Dan trailed his friend along the boardwalk but kept looking over his shoulder at the still smiling female. 'I think that I might try and get to know her a little better, Dixie. What you reckon?'

'Must be the starch, Dan,' Dix whispered.

'What you mean?'

'Reckon them clothes ain't the only thing that's a tad stiff, Dan!'

Dan chortled. 'There ain't no call for dirty talk, Dixie!'

'I ain't the one dribbling, Dan!'

Both men had almost reached the open doors of the saloon when they heard sounds of a ruckus coming from just inside the building. They paused just as a figure was thrown at hip height through the doorway. It landed beyond the boardwalk and rolled across the sand.

Dix took another step as a burly man tossed two pearl-handled guns at the figure lying face down between two horses.

Dix looked at Dan.

'That's Wild Bill!'

Both of them jumped down on to the sand, knelt and turned over the bruised and battered man they knew only too well.

'He's out for the count, Dixie.'

'I can see that.' Dix looked up at the figures standing in the doorway and gritted his teeth. He was about to rise when he felt a hand on his arm. Dix looked at his pal.

'Don't go off half-cocked, Dixie.'

Dan Shaw's words always doused the fire that still burned deep in the depths of Dix's soul. His head dropped until his chin touched his collarbone. He flexed his fingers and then saw the owner of the saloon charging through the lobby towards them.

'OK, pard,' Dix said to Dan.

Rufas Hardy forced his way past the largest of the men who had ejected Hickok and ran down to where the stunned gunfighter lay between the kneeling Dix and Dan. He cupped his sideburns in the palms of his hands as he looked down at the pitiful figure. He then turned his attention to Dix.

'Do you know him?' Hardy asked.

Dix simply nodded.

Hardy moved closer and leaned over. 'This is all my fault! I had to go out back and when I got there I heard the ruckus in the bar!'

Dan rubbed his freshly shaved face and squinted at the saloonkeeper. He could tell that Hardy felt genuine concern.

'Don't go blaming yourself. I've seen Bill drunk before but never quite as bad as this. A team of mules couldn't pull him away from a bottle when he's got the thirst gnawing at his craw.'

The female moved down from the boardwalk and looked at the man with the long brown mane of hair. Like all females Molly Doyle was interested in what she saw.

'So that's the famous Wild Bill Hickok?'

Hardy waved a hand at her.

'Go away, Molly! I've told you that we don't want your sort hanging around the Golden Spur.'

She smirked. 'That wife of yours will bankrupt you, Rufas.'

Hardy's eyes darted back at the saloon. His heart managed to keep beating normally when he realized that his wife was not close to the door. He returned his eyes to the female.

'Go away, Molly! Please? Bessie will kill me if she sees you. You know how she is.'

Dan and Dix heaved Hickok off the sand and balanced him between them as his hooded eyes began to blink.

'James Butler is mighty ripe,' Dix commented.

'We'd better take him to his room,' Dan said.

Dix was about to agree when over the shoulder of the tall Hickok he saw two men appear from a lane and then move along the boardwalk opposite.

'That ain't right!' Dix muttered. 'Leastways, it don't look right!'

Dan looked across Hickok at his friend. 'What ain't right, Dixie?'

'Since you seem to be a pal of James Butler's, you can help Dan take him up to his room.' Dix pulled Hardy close and gave him the burden of balancing the tall figure as he flicked the safety loops off his holstered guns.

As Dan and Hardy guided their dazed cargo up the steps to the porch, Dix squinted hard. The two men walked past the marshal's office and disappeared into the alley on the far side of the bank.

It was not the fact that there were two men walking close that had alerted Dix's honed instincts to there being something wrong, it was the fact that one of the men was bleeding whilst the other seemed to have his hand aimed at the base of the other's spine.

'Where you going, Dixie?' Dan called out.

There was no reply.

Tom Dix walked straight across the street towards the marshal's office. He stepped up on to the boards and then into the office.

Cooper and Sanders looked up and through the steam rising from their coffee mugs at the gunfighter.

'What's wrong, Dixie?' the marshal asked.

Dix strode to the deputy. 'Did you go to the banker's home and tell him what had happened, Bobby?'

Sanders nodded. 'Sure enough! I asked him if'n Brad had keys to the bank and he said that he didn't.'

'What does this banker look like?'

The young deputy lowered his mug. 'Jed is kinda small and fat and wears one of them silly hats they favour back East. You know the sort? Round on top and hardly no brim at all. You needs a big brim in this country.'

Cooper rose.

'What you asking about Jed for, Dixie?'

'Cos I think he just passed by, with a bigger man riding herd on him, Cooper,' Dix stated. 'I'm sure the bigger man had a gun on him.'

'Was they headed to the bank by any chance?' Marshal Cooper wrapped his gunbelt around his ample girth and buckled up. He moved round the desk and plucked his hat off the stand close to the door.

'Yep!' Dix answered.

Sanders leapt up. 'That might be the varmint who killed Brad, Marshal. Maybe he killed him so he could rob the bank but when he found that Brad didn't have no keys, he went and hunted down old Jed instead.'

Dix looked at Cooper and smiled.

'He's starting to get good at his job, Cooper.'

'It's in the blood, Dixie.'

All three men left the office and headed across the boardwalk towards the bank. They reached the alley and drew their weaponry.

Without another word they made their way into the shadows.

EIGHT

The alley was darker than the deepest of wells. Yet both men had moved along its narrow confines without hindrance to the back of the bank. The unlocking of the building's rear door had allowed the banker and the cowboy to enter quickly and without noise. Chance had pushed the door shut behind them and then shoved the older man forward. A dim amber light managed to filter through the gaps between the drapes which covered the building's every window. It traced through the darkness across the polished marble floor tiles straight to the door where the name of Jed Smith was painted in gold leaf upon its frosted glass panel.

Viciously Philo Chance dragged Smith by the collar across the floor of the bank towards the door. Unlike all the other doors within the fortified building this one was unlocked. Smith had always been a man with little if any imagination. He had

70

never considered it was necessary to lock his office door as he had never imagined that anyone might get into the bank, let alone reach his office. Chance forced the bank manager into the small windowless room and held him like a puppy by the scruff of his neck.

For a brief moment the cowboy stood and cast a keen gaze around the room. He pulled a match from his vest pocket and scratched it down the side of his chaps.

The flame flickered long enough for Chance to see the large safe standing proudly in the corner of the room. He strode to a lamp and touched its wick with the match.

Within a second the banker's office was bathed in the soft light only coal-tar could produce. Again Chance's eyes focused on the safe. He might have been drunk but he was sober enough to realize that its contents could allow him to live like a king for the rest of his days.

Chance tossed the spent match aside and grabbed hold of the shaking Smith. He put the large key ring into his hands once more.

'Open it!' the cowboy demanded.

Jed Smith felt the pistol as it hit him in his back. He stumbled towards the safe where every cent of the town's wealth was stored. Chance hovered over him like a vulture waiting for his meal to die. The cowboy was actually drooling at the thought of the money he was about to see and steal.

'Open the damn thing, Jed!' Chance snarled again. 'Do it fast, old-timer! I got me some living to do!'

'This is loco I tell you, Philo,' smith repeated. 'They'll hunt you down and kill you, boy! The whole town's money is in that safe. They won't let you get away with it.'

Without warning Chance raised his gun and smashed it across the small man's back. Smith screamed out in agony and staggered. He gave the cowboy a sideways glance and fell towards the safe.

'You better open it, Jed,' Chance warned as he trained the gun on the banker.

Smith wondered if Chance realized that all anyone had to do to open the safe was to insert the key into it and turn the damn thing. Could the cowboy be so stupid that he hadn't even thought of that? Did Philo actually believe that only the banker had the magical ability to open the safe?

Smith's fingers searched along the key ring until he located the right key. He inhaled deeply and then posted it into the small hole in the centre of the safe door.

Chance was eager. As soon as he heard the distinctive sound of the lock being released as the key was rotated he pushed the bank manager to the ground, grabbed hold of the safe's door handle and pulled it open.

'Holy Moses!' the cowboy gasped.

The cash was stacked neatly. Each denomination of bills in order of value. It filled more than half of the large interior of the safe. Below it was a lot of papers and on the very bottom shelf a glittering horde of golden coins, also stacked neatly.

'How much is in here, Jed?' Chance asked, in awe of the vision before him.

'About twenty thousand dollars,' Smith replied from the floor. He was staring at the blood on his clothing as the graze continued to drip blood from his cheek.

The cowboy looked around the office and then saw a canvas bag belonging to the banker in a corner. He pointed the barrel of his gun at it.

'Bring that bag over here fast, Jed,' Chance ordered. 'I'm gonna fill it with as much money as it'll hold!'

Smith wiped the blood from his mouth with his hands as his tongue located broken fragments of teeth stuck in his gums. He spat and heard them hit the solid tiles at his feet. His eyes looked at the cowboy. Suddenly the reality of the situation overwhelmed him.

There was no way that Chance would allow him to live once he had stolen the money. The cowboy had already told the banker that he had killed Brad the teller and that was information only a dead man could be entrusted with.

73

Smith's mind tried to think of a way of surviving this ordeal as he made his way to the large bag. With every step across the office floor his mind raced for a solution.

There was none.

The banker knew that he was only minutes away from being shot dead, yet he could not think.

He lifted the bag up.

'C'mon, Jed,' Chance urged. 'Git back here and fill this bag with all the money it can hold. Big bills. None of the small ones! I want all the tens and fives in this damn safe!'

Smith dropped to his knees in front of the open safe. Carefully he started to take the bills out and place them into the bag.

'You're gonna kill me, ain't you, Philo?' Smith managed to ask as blood dripped from his mouth.

'Why would I wanna kill you, Jed?'

'Why'd you kill Brad?'

'I ain't too sure why I done that.'

'You can't get away with this, boy!'

'Maybe.' The lamplight caught the expression on the cowboy's face as he turned and looked around the office. Philo Chance was smiling. Not the smile of a man who was amused. It was the smile of a man who had never been in control of his thoughts or his actions throughout his entire life.

It was the smile of a madman.

Smith had always wondered what it would be like

to be waiting to be hanged. What it might feel like to know that within minutes you would be dead.

Now he knew.

NINE

With the streetlights at their backs and nothing visible down into the alley beside the high-walled bank, the trio of men moved cautiously. They had seen one dead body since sunset and none of them wanted to add to the killer's tally. With one of his Colts drawn and ready for action Dix led Cooper and Sanders towards the rear of the building. The gunfighter found the door and paused. With the marshal and his deputy hanging over his shoulder, Tom Dix tried the doorknob with his free hand. To his surprise Dix found the door was not locked.

'I'll be damned!' Dix whispered. 'It ain't locked!'

Marshal Cooper leaned closer. 'You must be right, Dixie. There ain't no way that Jed would forget to lock up his bank. It must have bin him you seen being pushed along by that cowpoke. They gotta be inside right now.'

'Yeah,' Dix agreed.

'C'mon,' Sanders urged. 'Let's get in here and—'

Dix pushed his free hand to the lips of the young deputy and smothered the words. 'Quiet, Bobby! If I'm right there's someone inside here who might kill the banker if he hears us gabbing out here. Not another word. Savvy?'

The deputy nodded.

Elroy Cooper rested a hand on Tom Dix's shoulder and drew his attention.

'I oughta be the one who goes in there first, Dixie. That's what I'm paid for.'

Dix shook his head. 'Next time, Cooper. This might need some fast accurate shooting and that's what I'm good at.'

Reluctantly the marshal shrugged. 'OK.'

The veteran gunfighter knew that any sound from a creaking door would alert those within the building that someone was following. Dix knew that he would have to use every scrap of his seasoned skills if there were not to be another innocent man gunned down this night. He holstered his gun, carefully held the knob and then rested his other hand upon one of the door's panels. He lifted the door and then leaned upon it.

It opened without a sound.

Dix's eyes darted around the room through the narrow gap between the door and its frame. Then he eased the door inward and entered with the two lawmen to either side of him. All three paused and waited until their eyes fully adjusted to the dim light.

Bobby Sanders pointed the barrel of his gun towards the banker's office where the flickering light of the lamp danced across the door pane. But Dix had already seen it.

Dix nodded to the deputy. He drew one of his Colts and inhaled deeply. He then glanced at his companions in turn and waved his own weapon for them to spread out to either side of the half-open office door.

The sound of the laughing cowboy within the small office echoed all around the bank below the high vaulted ceiling. It drowned out the noise of the lawmen's boots as they crossed over the tiled floor towards their goal.

The marshal and the deputy had walked as quietly as they could until they were placed, as Dix had wanted, to both sides of the door. Dix had walked with tempered steps to the door itself.

The eyes of all three met.

Nothing was said.

There was no need for words. Each man instinctively knew what he had to do and was willing to face death in order to achieve their objective.

Dix leaned to his side and looked through the gap between the door and its frame. He could see the elated cowboy and the kneeling figure beside him.

He nodded.

Dix raised his boot and kicked out. The door

swung wide. As his foot found the floor inside the office, the gunfighter dropped on to one knee and cocked the hammer of his pistol. Cooper and Sanders moved into the room quickly behind him.

'Drop that hogleg!' Dix yelled out at Chance.

A startled Philo Chance turned his head. Then he stopped laughing.

His eyes saw the three men and narrowed in drunken fury. The tin stars of the two standing men danced in the glow of lamplight but it was the man who knelt who drew his attention the most. Chance had long lost any fear of Cooper but the stranger was another matter.

Men like Tom Dix looked dangerous and even a half-witted cowboy could sense that.

Philo Chance blinked hard and feverishly swung around to face them. The gun in his hand was already cocked and ready.

'Drop it, Philo!' Marshal Cooper called out.

'I'll drop you, not my gun!' The cowboy squeezed the trigger just as he saw a trio of smoke plumes erupt from the guns of the men in the doorway. The bank rocked as the thunderous noise reverberated against its walls.

Shot after shot rang out.

The acrid stench of choking gunsmoke quickly filled the office as fingers squeezed on triggers again and again. Bullets crossed the office in both directions. Within a few seconds the distance that

79

separated the men was clogged with the dense fog of gunplay.

As a red-hot taper of lead passed a few inches from his left cheek, Dix switched guns and returned fire.

Men cried out in pain as lead hit them. Then there were no more shots coming from where the cowboy had been standing. Dix shook the hot casings from his gun and reloaded the weapon.

Unable to see anything as the smoke of a score of bullets blanketed the middle of the room, Dix raised a hand.

'I think we got him, boys!'

For a few endless seconds the gunfighter just chewed on the gunsmoke and listened.

'Yep. I reckon we got him OK.' Dix said again.

Then Dix realized that something was very wrong behind him. His head quickly turned to check the lawmen. He screwed up his eyes. He did not like what he saw. Bobby Sanders was still standing but he was holding his arm. Blood ran down from the ugly wound just above his elbow.

'I'm hit, Mr Dix,' the deputy said.

'Easy, Bobby,' Dix answered.

'I'm OK!' Sanders gulped hard and looked to where the marshal stood. 'But Uncle Elroy don't look so good.'

Dix's eyes darted to Cooper. To his horror he saw the marshal leaning against the woodwork of the doorframe. The Colt .45 hung on his index finger as he gasped for air. Then the gun fell and bounced on the floor. Dix rose to his feet and went to steady the burly man. Cooper coughed and looked down at his protruding stomach. His shirt was stained crimson. Three black holes were dotted amid the gore.

'I bin gut-shot, Dixie!' Cooper managed to mutter before he slid down the wall. 'I can't feel my legs!'

'Cooper!' Dix held Cooper's shoulders. Blood was pumping from the wounds in the man's belly. Within hardly more than a heartbeat it had spread down over the man's thighs.

Elroy Cooper's eyes flickered and then rolled up under their lids. The marshal fell to his side. Dix eased the limp body down as though it were made of eggshell.

'Uncle Elroy?' Sanders cried out.

'He can't hear you no more, Bobby,' Dix said.

The deputy managed to walk to where the body lay. He fell down and began to sob.

Dix released his grip on the dead man, turned and stared across the room. He wiped the blood on his hands down his new shirt and snorted like an enraged bull. The gunsmoke was dispersing fast and Dix could see the cowboy on his side with the gun still gripped in his hand.

He leaned down. He could see the banker crawling fearfully away to a corner of the room. Dix did not speak.

Furiously he pulled his guns from their holsters

again and cocked their hammers until they fully locked. It was as if a volcano had erupted inside the gunfighter's mind. He continued to stare at the cowboy who lay on his side. Then he saw Chance's leg move.

The cowboy was still alive.

Dix spun the guns on his fingers expertly. 'I should have just plugged that bastard and not given him time to open up, Bobby,' Dix drawled angrily. 'I made me a real bad mistake and I gotta fix it!'

'W-what you doing, Mr Dix?' Bobby Sanders asked innocently as he cradled the body of his uncle.

Dix did not answer. Every ounce of his attention was on the cowboy who had killed the marshal. He had never known such fury before. It burned into his very soul.

'Mr Dix?'

As if in a trance Dix began to walk toward the cowboy. His guns were trained on Philo Chance.

'I made me a mistake that cost a man his life.' Dix repeated his words and steadied his weaponry. 'A good man. This *hombre* ain't never gonna kill nobody else! Tom Dix will make damn sure of that, Bobby!'

'Mr Dix?'

Dix did not hear the deputy's words. All he could hear was the thundering of his heart as he closed in on the cowboy.

'He ain't ever gonna kill nobody again!'

TEN

It was like being gripped by a grizzly bear. Dix felt the arms encircling him from behind and dragging him backwards. The arms tightened their hold. The pair of matched Colt .45s fell from the hands of the veteran gunfighter as the grip tightened. Dix tried to fight but he was helpless against the powerful attack. For a few endless seconds the gunfighter wrestled against being subdued.

'Dixie!' The familiar voice yelled into his ears.

Suddenly Dix realized that it was his sidekick who had stopped him from squeezing on his triggers and blasting the injured cowboy into the next world.

'Dan?'

Dan Shaw released his grip and allowed his saddle partner to stumble away. The retired marshal stood firm and stared at the startled face. Dix cast his eyes upon him in disbelief.

'What in tarnation are you doing?' Dix yelled.

For a few moments the retired lawman said nothing. He watched as the fire inside his pal ebbed and then disappeared from the wrinkled face.

'You OK now, Dixie?' Dan asked.

Dix blinked hard, then glanced back at the cowboy on the floor close to the safe. He raised a hand and pointed at Chance.

'That vermin killed Cooper, Dan!' he exclaimed loudly. 'I was gonna send him to Hell. Why'd you stop me?'

Dan stepped closer to his friend. Their eyes met.

'Why'd I stop you? You were plumb loco with anger, Dixie! I recall you being like that a long time back and it got you into a whole heap of trouble. You can't kill anyone like this. Not even scum like him! You're better than that, Dixie.'

'Who'd know?' Dix spat.

'You'd know, Dixie,' Dan retorted. 'And I know that when you cooled down you'd not be able to live with yourself.'

Dix sighed heavily. He paced around the office and kicked the gun from Philo Chance's hand. It skidded across the tiled floor to where the terrified Jed Smith was huddled in a corner. The gunfighter paused and stared into the banker's wide-open eyes. He saw the terror which carved into the man's face. Dix turned and looked back at Dan.

'What you intending we do?' Dix asked.

'We're gonna lock him up all legal like.' Dan

walked to the cowboy on the floor and stooped. He plucked the other gun from its holster and rammed it into his own belt. He straightened up and returned his attention to his pal. 'Then we get a district judge in here and let a jury decide.'

Dix held out a helping hand to the banker and eased the man off the floor. He walked to where his own guns lay, bent down and picked them both up. He holstered the Colts and gave the ceiling a long hard look.

Dix raised an eyebrow. 'What if they find this bastard innocent, Dan? What then?'

Dan Shaw almost smiled.

'If that happens we'll have to buy ourselves a rope, Dixie.'

Dix sighed heavily once more. 'I wish I believed you but we've ridden together for too long for me to fall for that. You might be retired but there ain't no way that you'll ever be anything except a lawman.'

Dan nodded. 'Damn right! There was a time when I could have shot you and not followed the law, Dixie. I'm sure glad I let myself calm down long enough to see who and what you really are.'

Dix glanced at the deputy, who was sitting on the floor next to the body of Marshal Cooper, near the office door. Bobby Sanders was soaked to the skin in his uncle's blood. His eyes seemed glazed in the light of the lamp as they stared out into a place where nightmares destroyed the hopes of the innocent.

'Are we gonna hold this varmint prisoner 'til the judge shows up, Dan?' Dix asked. 'Cos there ain't no way young Bobby is in any state to do so.'

'Yep,' Dan replied firmly.

'Just thought I'd ask,' Dix shrugged.

'We have to do this, Dixie,' Dan urged.

'Reckon so, pard,' the gunfighter agreed.

Dan patted his partner's shoulder. 'I'll go send a wire to get a judge sent here as soon as possible. I'll get old Joe to come and take a look at Bobby and our prisoner and then we'll cart that cowpoke off to the jail and lock him up.'

'You better get that liveryman to come and take care of Cooper as well, Dan boy,' Dix added.

'Yeah,' Dan breathed hard. 'That too.'

Tom Dix watched as his friend left the office. He listened to the sound of the boots as they resounded on the marble-tiled floor of the bank. Then he saw the frail ashen-featured banker by the door. His expression resembled that of the deputy. It was as though their brains had been fried by the Devil himself. They had seen what death looked like and neither man could cope with the vision which would forever haunt them.

Dix led Smith to a padded leather chair and helped the man sit down. On a bookcase he saw a bottle of brandy and a few glass tumblers. He filled three and handed one to Smith.

'T-thanks,' Smith muttered.

Dix picked up another and downed the strong drink. He then took the last glass to the deputy and forced Sanders to accept it.

'Drink this, Bobby,' he ordered.

The injured deputy did as he was told and coughed as its fire burned down inside him.

'What was that stuff, Dix?' he asked as tears gradually filled his eyes.

'Something to help your pain, Bobby,' Dix returned his attention to the cowboy. The man had turned over and was staring at him with a crooked smile carved across his face.

Philo Chance raised his head off the floor and looked hard at the gunfighter.

'You really think that you can hold me in jail, old-timer?'

Dix nodded.

'Yep. But I'd still prefer to kill you instead.'

'Do you have any idea who I am?'

'Yep. You're the bastard who's gonna have his neck stretched for killing Marshal Cooper.'

The cowboy stopped talking.

Hired gun Will Fontaine steered his dust-caked mount up to the hitching rail outside the Broken Bottle saloon and pulled back on his reins. The exhausted animal stopped and lowered its head. Fontaine's eyes were like those of a hunting eagle as they surveyed the long boardwalks on both sides of

Main Street. There were still scores of people filling and spilling out of the five saloons dotted along the otherwise subdued thoroughfare. The gunman sat and watched with one hand on his saddle horn whilst the other rested on the grip of one of his guns. He had expected Gun Fury to be busier. He liked crowds for they gave men of his profession cover. The fewer people, the harder it was to move around unnoticed.

Will Fontaine made his living by selling his deadly gun skills to the highest bidder. That made him many enemies. Enemies who did not comply with the unwritten code he and his ilk lived by. Enemies who would seek revenge by any means they thought might offer them the chance of survival against someone as fast on the draw as he was.

Only when satisfied that none of the people posed any threat to him did Fontaine ease himself up off his saddle and step down to the sand. The thin cigar gripped between his teeth was well chewed and had kept his mind occupied for the previous three hours of his long ride. Yet he showed no sign of ever trying to light it.

Fontaine flicked the long ends of reins over the hitching pole and tied them firmly. He stepped up on to the boardwalk and gave the street another careful scrutiny. For men of his occupation lived and died by the gun. They knew that when you were fast most men would not face you. They would wait until they could take aim at your spine.

'Going inside, stranger?' Molly Doyle asked, sauntering up to the tall man dressed in black leather and a thin coating of trail dust. 'I could give you a good time if you've got the time and the money.'

Fontaine looked down at the female as she strolled from the shadows into the light which glowed forth from the saloon. He said nothing for a moment but kept watching her. Then he moved and rested a hand upon the top of the swing door. He looked inside the Broken Bottle before returning his eyes to the sweet-smelling female.

'Much obliged for the kind offer of friendship, ma'am.' Fontaine said with a touch of his hat brim. 'But I'm kinda trail sore and got me some business to deal with before I can enjoy the obvious pleasures you have in abundance.'

Molly stepped closer. The man towered over her, as did most of the other men in Gun Fury. Even with three-inch heels on her buttoned-up shoes she still barely managed to reach five feet in height. But height had nothing to do with her profession. Her eyelashes fluttered as her gloved index finger toyed with the tails of his bandanna.

'You talk real sweet, stranger. What they call you?'

'Will Fontaine, ma'am,' he replied.

Molly had heard the name before. She looked him up and down the way a cowboy inspected a prime steer, then smiled.

'Are you the gunslinger?'

'One and the same, ma'am,' Fontaine replied. 'I'm surprised that you've heard of me.'

'My name's Molly.'

'A pretty name for a real pretty lady.'

She edged closer. She could smell the alluring mixture of his aroma. It was sweat and the scent of the wide-open range and she liked it. She knew the difference between the stale sweat of the bone idle and the honest sweat of someone who has worked hard.

'Two bucks and you can talk sweet to me all night, Will!'

He was tempted. It had been weeks since he had last enjoyed the pleasures of a woman and he was hungry for more. But there was business to get sorted before he could relax and allow himself the pleasures she seemed to be offering.

'I'm surely tempted but I have to get something done first, Molly,' he explained.

'What could be so important, Will?' Her fingers found a gap between his shirt buttons and teased at the hair on his chest.

Again Fontaine looked all around the street. A few men were falling out of the Lucky Dice and heading across the street towards the Golden Spur. When satisfied they were harmless drunks his eyes focused on her again.

'Do you happen to know a man called Wild Bill Hickok?'

Molly smiled.

'Every girl with blood in her veins knows of Wild Bill, handsome,' Molly said. 'Why?'

'He's my business.' Fontaine admitted.

Molly looked hard at the man's face. She tried to read his thoughts but it was impossible. He was like a poker-player and did not give anything away in his expression.

'You got business with Bill?'

'Kinda,' Fontaine nodded before looking inside the saloon again.

'You ain't bin hired to call him out, have you?'

He simply smiled. 'Maybe.'

'It ain't worth wasting the lead, Will,' Molly explained. 'I seen me a lotta gunmen but Wild Bill's on a drunk. He was thrown out of the Golden Spur earlier. He couldn't even find his guns let alone draw the things.'

Fontaine grinned. 'Then if I was here to square up to him it seems I've picked the right time.'

'I thought you said that he was your business?' Molly was confused.

Fontaine glanced along the boardwalk. 'I have to meet up with someone else first, Molly. Wild Bill is just a bonus.'

Molly stared hard up at him. 'I don't understand.'

He touched her cheek. 'Don't go fretting, Molly. I'd hate you to get any wrinkles on that pretty face of yours.'

91

For the first time she did not trust the man she was trying to persuade to use her services.

She took a step back. 'What's the name of the other man you've come to Gun Fury to see? Has someone here hired you to draw down on Wild Bill?'

Fontaine did not answer.

Molly pulled at the bandanna. His head lowered and she looked into his eyes. He looked down into her cleavage.

'Two bucks, Will! Just two measly bucks.'

Fontaine took her wrists in his gloved hands. 'Where's Hickok right now, Molly?'

Her head tilted. 'Why?'

'Tell me where he's at.' Fontaine's voice suddenly lost the smooth charm she had at first been drawn to. Now it was a low growl. 'Tell me!'

Molly flicked her head back and stared through her long lashes at him. She went to pull away but his grip tightened around her almost white wrists.

'Let go of me,' she demanded.

He squeezed even harder. 'Where is he holed up?'

'You're hurting me, Will,' Molly said breathlessly.

'Then answer my question.' Fontaine began to turn her arms as he held on to her wrists.

She could have screamed but Molly Doyle was made of sterner stuff and refused to let him see her pain. Her eyes narrowed and she gritted her teeth.

'Go to hell!'

Fontaine raised both eyebrows. He admired spirit

and she was loaded with it. He released her, turned away, pushed the saloon's swing doors inward and entered the Broken Bottle.

'Reckon I will someday, Molly,' Fontaine said over his broad shoulder.

Molly Doyle stood silently on the boardwalk and watched the tall handsome man as he strode across the sawdust to the long counter and gestured to the barkeep.

For the first time in many a long year she did not know what to do next. She walked back into the shadows to find a place where she might be able to think.

As she walked and rubbed her bruised wrists she saw the light in the marshal's office.

ELEVEN

The telegraph office stood abandoned at the very edge of Gun Fury without any sign of life in its weathered boarding. Like half the other buildings in the town it had been left to rot as the settlement's fortunes withered. Mustering the decades of knowledge he had gained as a lawman, Dan Shaw had located the jobless telegraph operator and taken him to the ramshackle building. With a shining new silver dollar in his hand Milburn Davis had willingly followed the silver-haired man to the place where he had worked for over five years.

Dan forced the warped door open and fought his way through the cobwebs and dust until he lit upon the small machine he had prayed would have been left when the telegraph company deserted to the distant railhead. Davis brushed the dust from the desk and then cranked up the small dynamo at his feet. He started to tap until he received a return message.

'Well damn it all!' Davis gasped in surprise. 'I reckon we're still hooked up to the main line over in El Paso!'

Dan struck a match and lit a candle beside the operator.

'What ya want me to say, Mr Dan?' Davis asked. 'I can get straight through to the authorities there.'

Dan rubbed his jaw. 'Tell them that Marshal Cooper has been murdered and his deputy is wounded, Mil. Also tell them we've got the culprit and are awaiting a circuit judge to get down here.'

Davis began to tap with expert precision. 'Anything else?'

'Tell them that retired US Marshal Dan Shaw is holding the prisoner in the town jail until the judge arrives.'

Milburn Davis continued to tap the keyboard.

Dan Shaw made his way back to the door. He paused and glanced back at Davis.

'Stay there until they answer, Mil. Then bring it to me at the marshal's office as fast as them legs of yours can carry you, OK?'

'No problem, Mr Dan,' Davis nodded.

Philo Chance had been wounded but there was no way that the bullets which Dix and the two lawmen had fired had come anywhere close to ending the cowboy's worthless existence. He had been lucky and had twisted and then fallen to the floor before any of the shots could find his substantial torso. Every shot had caught the man in his muscular left arm; then the choking gunsmoke had shielded him from his assailants' view and the rest of the bullets. A half-hour later in the Gun Fury jailhouse, Barber Joe had dug three lumps of lead out of the prisoner's arm before pouring half a bottle of iodine over the catgut stitches.

Somehow the defiant cowboy killer had managed to stay awake as the barber had worked. He had not stopped taunting the steely eyed Dix throughout the crude operation.

Dix kept the barrel of one of his guns trained on Chance until he escorted the barber out of the cell and turned the key in its stiff lock.

'My pa will kill all of you!' Chance ranted as Dix closed the door to the marshal's office and eased the hammer back down on his Colt.

Joe Benson accepted a cup of coffee from Bobby Sanders and rested a hip on the edge of the desk.

'How's the arm, Bobby?' the barber asked.

Sanders placed the palm of one hand over the bandage. 'It's darn good thanks to you, Joe.'

Dix picked up a cloth and gripped the handle of the coffee pot. He poured the well-brewed beverage into a cup and lowered the pot back on top of the stove. He blew into the steam and stared out of the window at the street.

'You sure that you're OK, Bobby?' Dix asked the deputy without taking his eyes from the street. 'I figure you'd be better off at home in bed.'

'I'm OK, Dix,' Sanders insisted.

Dix tilted his head and looked at the youngster.

'I'm sorry, Bobby.'

'There ain't no call,' Sanders said.

Dix nodded and then sipped at the coffee. 'That cowpoke sure made a lot of threats in there, Joe. Any reason why I ought to be troubled?'

Benson made a face. It was the sort of expression men always made when unsure of telling the truth for fear of worrying or upsetting the questioner.

'His pa is a man to be reckoned with, Dixie,' the barber said at last. 'A real monster of a man who gets what he wants whatever it is. Philo is just one of his sons but the craziest by a mile.'

'That's right, Dixie,' Sanders nodded. 'Pop Chance is a mean bastard and no mistake.'

Dix sat down in the marshal's chair and placed the cup on the ink blotter before him. He stared at the man who was far more than a barber.

'Who is his pa, Joe?'

'Nobody knows his real handle! They call him Pop Chance.' Benson continued, 'He got two other sons named Seth and Bodine. They also got at least a dozen cowhands. They run a spread about five miles east called the Circle C.'

'And they're all loco,' Sanders offered. 'But Philo

97

is the worst of a bad bunch.'

'They ain't never bin brought to justice in all the time I've lived here, Dix,' Benson said. 'They're a fearful bunch of killers who just ride roughshod over anyone who gets in their way. When they find out about Philo being locked up in this jail, they'll come looking for him.'

Dix's eyes darted to the deputy. 'They ain't never bin brought to book?'

Bobby Sanders shook his head. 'Nope. Even Uncle Elroy wouldn't go up against them. They'd burn the whole town down if anyone ever stood up against them.'

Dix looked into his cup. The steam drew his thoughts.

'So holding Philo here is kinda dangerous?'

'Suicidal,' Benson corrected.

'I always like a challenge.'

The office door opened. Dix swung around on his chair, stood and instinctively drew one of his guns. The gunfighter stared at the female who paused in the doorway. He returned the gun to its holster and sighed as Molly entered and closed the door behind her. He was about to speak but she moved to the window and peered over the green drape which covered its lower half.

'Where's Cooper?' Molly asked without turning.

Bobby shook his lowered head. 'Uncle Elroy's dead, Molly.'

She turned. 'Cooper's dead? How?'

Dix stepped closer to her. 'We had us a ruckus in the bank earlier, ma'am. The marshal was belly shot.'

'Philo Chance done it,' Benson said.

Molly looked truly upset. She walked to the nearest chair and sat down. Her face disappeared into her hands and she began to sob.

Joe Benson lowered his cup and placed it on the desk. He eyed the two other men and then left the office.

Dix was about to speak when he saw the bruises on her thin wrists. He crouched beside her. His eyes focused on the bruising. He could clearly see the unmistakable marks of fingers on her pale flesh.

'Who hurt you, Molly?'

She looked at Dix. Tears did not diminish her beauty but only enhanced it to the veteran gunfighter.

'You ever heard of an *hombre* named Will Fontaine, Dixie?'

Dix nodded slowly.

'Yep.'

'He just rode in and he's gunning for Wild Bill!' Molly said.

Dix bit his lip.

'Who's Will Fontaine, Dixie?' the deputy asked.

Dix swallowed hard.

'A gunfighter, Bobby.'

'Like you?'

Dix shook his head. 'Nope. They say he's faster than anyone who ever lived.'

Molly looked at Dix. 'Wild Bill ain't in no state to face anyone, Dixie! You seen the poor critter earlier! If Fontaine draws on him, it'll be murder.'

Dix inhaled hard.

He knew she was right.

TWELVE

Horace Steed was the last of the town's council members still to remain in office in Gun Fury. He had taken the mantle of mayor because no one else wanted the meaningless title. The man was as run down and weatherworn as the town itself. He paraded about its streets in clothes which no longer retained the splendour they'd had when they were first made for him during Gun Fury's heyday. Patches and frayed edges displayed the obvious to onlookers.

Yet for all his blustering and ability to create one pointless new law after another, few if any ever listened to him.

Steed came from a time when the council was easily bribed by the railroad company to do exactly as they wished. Nobody had ever forgotten his betrayal or the fact that he, along with the other now absent politicians, had fattened their own wallets at the expense of everyone else.

101

The rotund figure had heard of the fatal slayings earlier and as the sun rose and cast its light across the bleached dwellings on the edge of town he walked down Main Street towards the marshal's office with another hastily drafted sheet of paper in his hand.

Dan Shaw had slept little during what had remained of the night after he had received the message from El Paso. He as well as Dix had remained inside the office waiting for the trouble they knew would inevitably come as sure as the sun would rise, no matter what.

Both men heard the creaking of the boardwalk outside as Steed forced his well-fed body along towards the door of the marshal's office. They watched the brass knob turn as the mayor vainly tried to enter.

Dix rose from the cot and walked to the door. 'We got us some company, Dan.'

Dan stood up from the chair and glanced at his friend. He had seen the man walk past the window from the marshal's desk.

'It's just a fat old man, Dixie.'

Dix raised a hand to the bolt at the top of the door.

'Reckon it's Pop Chance?' he asked before sliding its bolt free.

Dan shook his head. 'I doubt it. I reckon Pop Chance will arrive with his other sons and cowhands in tow and make one hell of a noise when they do.'

'Yeah.' Dix released the bolt and the stepped back as the mayor blustered in.

'This is an outrage,' Steed said waving the sheet of paper in his hand. 'Who, might I ask, are you?'

The two men stepped close to the red-faced creature, whom they had never seen before.

'Who are you?' Dix stooped and asked.

Steed looked up at the gunfighter. He saw the well-maintained shooting rig with its matched pair of holstered Colts and then decided to swallow hard.

'I'm Horace Steed. I'm the mayor of Gun Fury.'

'Well howdy, Horace.' Dan touched his temple. 'How can me and my pard help you?'

'I'm reliably informed that you have Philo Chance locked up in one of the cells,' Steed boomed and waved the paper under Dan's nose. 'I have a law here which prohibits such actions by men who have no legal right to do so.'

'Well ain't that a funny thing, Horace?' Dan Shaw picked up the small sheet of paper he had been given hours earlier by Milburn Davis. He shook it under the nose of the mayor. 'I got me a paper too. This 'un's from El Paso and it gives me the authority to act as marshal until the district judge gets into town.'

Steed went even redder.

'Who are you, sir?'

'I'm Dan Shaw,' Dan smiled. 'Acting marshal of Gun Fury.'

'I don't care what that wire states! Release Philo at once, Shaw,' Steed insisted. 'Otherwise we'll have us the whole wrath of the Circle C down on us. They'll burn the town to the ground. You can't go up against the Chance clan and survive.'

Dan Shaw smiled again.

'I can and I will.'

'The streets will flow with the blood of innocents,' Steed proclaimed. 'It shall be on your head.'

'Our heads, Horace,' Dix interrupted. 'Me and Dan are in this to the end. Seems to me like this Chance family are a tad overdue to be brought to book.'

'And who are you?' Steed asked. 'Another marshal?'

'Nope,' Dix said bluntly. 'I used to be gunfighter.'

Horace Steed waved his arms around frantically and stormed to the door. He paused and looked at the two men who were also looking back at him.

'Mark my words. This will be the end of Gun Fury. You men are gonna destroy an entire town.'

Dix ambled slowly to the blustering mayor. 'You're wrong there, Horace. Me and Dan are gonna make sure that justice is finally served on them Chance varmints.'

'You are fools,' Steed exclaimed. 'Blind fools!'

Dan marched to the man in the suit that no longer fitted his ample frame. He raised a finger and pointed it.

'Marshal Cooper was killed last night. A bank teller was also gunned down. Philo Chance is gonna pay for that, whatever you think.'

Steed stood open-mouthed as the sheet of paper with his latest law scribbled upon it was torn from his sweating hand and then ripped to shreds in front of him.

'I'm the law in Gun Fury now, Steed.' Dan said firmly. 'If them Circle C bastards want to go up against me and Dixie, then they'll be taking on the law.'

'Fools!' Steed spat and thundered away as best his short fat legs could manage.

Dix gave a long sigh. 'You reckon he might just be right about us being fools, Dan?'

Just as Dan was about to reply both men heard the sound of shouting coming from the cells beyond the sturdy door which separated the jailhouse from the office.

'Sounds like Philo's starting to shout up a storm again, Dan,' Dix remarked.

'That ain't Philo,' Dan said with a twinkle in his eyes.

Both men grinned and walked across the floor to the door. Dix took the ring of keys from a nail on the wall and opened the wooden door to reveal the two cells.

Philo Chance was on his cot in one cell snoring but the occupant of the other was standing with his hands gripping the cell bars.

'What the hell is going on? Who locked me up in here?'

Dan and Dixie walked to the man and could not hide their amusement at the sight. Hickok's eyes widened when he recognized the two men.

'Dan? Dixie?' he gasped.

'Wild Bill.' Dan nodded.

'Howdy, James Butler,' Dix said as he slowly searched the key ring for the one which would unlock the cell door. 'How'd you get in here?'

'You long string of bacon must have locked me in here, Dixie,' Hickok raged. 'Why?'

Dan edged closer. 'We figured it would be a real sure way of making sure that Will Fontaine wouldn't gun you down in your hotel room, Bill.'

'Fontaine?' Hickok blinked hard. 'Who the hell is he?'

'A gunfighter trying to make a name for himself, James Butler,' Dix explained. 'But the strange thing is that someone hired him to come here and kill you.'

'What?' Hickok ran his fingers through his mane of long hair and tried to understand. 'Speak American, Dixie! What's going on here? And how come you're both here in this god-forsaken town? I don't understand any of this nonsense!'

Dix continued to pretend he could not find the correct key that would release the tall flamboyant man from the jail cell.

'Why'd you send for us, James Butler?'

Hickok stared at Dix. 'I never sent for you!'

'Yes you did,' Dan argued.

'I never sent for you,' Hickok yelled.

Dan pulled a crumpled telegraph message from his pants pocket and showed it to Hickok. Hickok shook his head and rubbed his eyes.

'I can't read that. My eyes ain't working right. Get me a drink. Get me a bottle of whiskey. Get me out of here.'

Dix stopped looking for the right key. 'No more liquor for you, James Butler. Not for a while, anyways.'

Hickok grabbed the bars and shook them. 'Get me some whiskey, Dixie. I'll kill you if'n you don't!'

'We'll be back with some coffee,' Dan said.

Both men turned away from Hickok. They walked back to the stout wooden office door.

'Where the hell are you going?' Hickok shouted.

Dix looked at the famous features. 'We need you sober, James Butler. Not drunk and wallowing in your own filth. Sober! We got trouble headed at us and I don't know if me and Dan can handle it without you.'

Hickok stopped shouting.

The words had cut into his befuddled mind like a straight razor. The man who was a legend sat down on the cot inside his cell and watched as the door closed.

There was trouble brewing? They need my help? A thousand questions burned through the fumes of all the whiskey he had consumed. He inhaled deeply and then caught the scent of his own dirty body and clothes.

Hickok raised his head and shouted once more.

'OK! I give up. Bring me a pot of coffee, Dixie. I'll drink the putrid brew. I'll drink as much of the foul stuff as you can make. But get me my bag from the hotel first.'

The door opened and Dan looked into the cell at Hickok.

'What you need your bag for, Bill?'

'It's got my clean clothes in it, Dan boy,' Hickok said quietly. 'My fancy town clothes. My gunfighting clothes.'

'I'll tell Joe the barber to make sure he's got a bath ready for you, Wild Bill,' Dan smiled.

Hickok raised a hand and saluted the man. 'But I didn't send you boys a wire to come here! I'm sure of that, Dan.'

Dan rubbed his whiskers.

'Then who did and why?'

The question went unanswered.

Hickok gestured to the retired marshal. Dan returned to the cell and looked down at the seated figure.

'What you want now, Bill?'

'You ain't got a cigar on you, have you?'

Dan smiled. 'I'll get you a box.'

As Dan walked past Dix he whispered, 'I reckon he's sobered up already, Dixie.'

Dix poured out a cup of coffee, then glanced at the office wall clock. It was almost six.

'I sure hope so! Ranchers get up darn early and it ain't a long ride from the Circle C to Gun Fury.'

Dan nodded.

'I wonder how long we've got before they find out about Philo being locked up in here?'

Suddenly both men heard the noise out in the street. The sound of horses being ridden by enraged cowboys screaming at the tops of their lungs. Guns were being fired in all directions.

Both men looked out of the window at the few early risers running for their lives. Dust floated past and then they saw the horses and their riders draw rein outside the office.

Dix lowered the coffee cup.

'I'll get James Butler.'

Dan said nothing as his partner ran towards the cell with the keys. His eyes narrowed and were fixed upon the burly horseman with the white beard who held a scattergun in his hands.

THIRTEEN

Dix had just reached the cells when his attention was drawn to his partner back in the office at the door which led out on to Main Street and to the ten dishevelled riders who sat chewing on their own dust. The seasoned gunfighter paused as his heart raced inside his shirt. Dix knew that his saddle pal had never been as good with a gun as he himself had always been, yet Dan had something which Dix had never possessed. The retired lawman had blind faith in the law and its ability to protect him.

Dan looked over his shoulder at Dix and then drew his trusty .45 from its holster. He cocked its hammer until the Colt was primed, then held on to the doorknob.

'If they kill me, Dixie,' Dan called out loud

enough for half the street to overhear, 'shoot Philo dead!'

'Yeah?' Dix responded.

'You heard me, pard!' The man who had lived most of his days as a lawman twisted the doorknob and jerked it swiftly towards him. The array of horses shied. Dan screwed up his eyes and defiantly walked out beneath the porch overhang. There were ten of them. Each of them as sun-weathered as the next. Each of them had enough weaponry to start a small war and they all looked as though they knew how to handle themselves. These riders might be cowboys now, but Dan suspected that more than a few of them had once had far more lethal professions.

Dan squared up to them in the porch shadows. He held his gun at hip level as Dix had taught him. Its barrel was aimed straight up at the most fearsome-looking of the bunch: the man who called himself Pop Chance. The man with the whitest beard he had ever encountered.

'You got a problem, *amigo*?' Dan asked boldly.

'I'll kill ya!' Pop Chance went to move his scattergun when he saw the Colt being raised and trained on him.

'I'd not move another muscle, Chance, if I was you. Unless you hanker for going to Boot Hill before your time, that is.'

The horsemen who surrounded Pop Chance all

looked to their leader as though expecting him to defy the words of Dan Shaw. Yet Pop Chance had not lived as long as he had by being dumb. He had no doubt in his mind that the man before him was not bluffing.

Chance lowered the rifle until it rested across his saddle horn.

'Who the hell are you, stranger?' Chance growled. 'What you doing in Cooper's office?'

'I'm the new marshal,' Dan answered. 'Your boy killed the old one last night.'

'You lying bastard!' Chance snarled. 'Why would he kill Cooper?'

'Why would he try to rob the bank?' Dan snapped back.

Pop Chance adjusted himself on his saddle. 'Let my Philo go, Marshal, right now.'

'Nope.' Dan licked his lips.

The other riders seemed to be getting anxious. Bodine Chance edged his mount closer to his father's and leaned across the distance between them.

'We gonna confab all day, Pa? Or is we gonna kill this old runt and take Philo home?'

Dan stepped closer to the edge of the boardwalk. 'If any of you draw down on me my partner has orders to blow Philo's head off his shoulders, Pop.'

'Who's your partner?' Chance queried.

'Tom Dix.'

Pop Chance sucked in his cheeks. Deep lines

appeared on his brow just below his hat line. He had heard of Dix and what he had heard troubled the old rancher. He breathed heavily and looked to his men on either side of him.

'Keep them hoglegs holstered,' he ordered. 'This old man is loco enough to be telling the truth.'

'He's bluffing, Pa,' Seth Chance said.

'Maybe he is and maybe he ain't, Seth boy,' Pop Chance muttered. 'But I ain't taking the risk.'

'But we come here to get Philo and take him home, Pa.'

'Ain't much point taking Philo home with his head in a saddle-bag, boy,' Chance shouted. 'Is there?'

Dan Shaw felt the sweat trail down his spine beneath his shirt. He was thankful the cowboys could not see it for they might just call his bluff if they did.

Pop Chance gathered his reins in his right hand and pulled his horse's head up. He stared at the defiant lawman and nodded slowly to him.

'You got until sundown tonight to release my boy, Marshal.'

'And if I don't?'

'Then we start burning and killing,' Chance replied. 'It won't take long for the good folks of Gun Fury to see that they got themselves a real troublesome lawman holding my Philo in jail. I reckon they'll want to string you up as bad as I do by midnight.'

113

Dan kept perfectly still. He continued to hold his right hand straight out with its gun aimed at the leader of the cowboys. His face remained totally still.

Chance backed his horse away from the hitching rail, turned its head and then spurred. The rest of the Circle C rode behind him. Dust rose high into the air from the hoofs of the ten mounts as Dan lowered his gun and sighed with relief.

He walked back into the office just as Dix and Hickok left the jailhouse.

'You look like death warmed up,' Dix remarked.

'That was the best hand of poker you ever played, Dan,' Hickok praised. 'Even I believed you.'

Dan shook his head and sat down. He placed the gun on the desk and then looked at his hand. It was shaking as the true magnitude of what he had just done sank into him. He felt sick and had a pain in his lower back.

'Leastways I bought us a little time.' Dan gave a sigh.

Hickok picked up the full coffee cup and downed its contents in one swallow. He refilled it and then repeated the action before looking down at himself.

'I'm gonna go get me a bath, boys,' he declared.

Dix nodded. 'I'll go and get your bag from the Golden Spur, James Butler.'

'Check there ain't a bottle of rye hidden inside it, Dixie,' Dan smiled.

114

Hickok looked at the seated man. It was the look which had been emblazoned upon the jacket covers of a hundred or more dime novels.

Hickok saw his holstered guns hanging from the hat stand and retrieved them. 'Don't go fretting none, old friend. You've bitten off more than either of you can chew and it's gonna take handsome Wild Bill Hickok's mastery to pull your bacon out of the fire once again.'

Dan nodded in agreement.

'Sober?' Dix grinned.

'My eyes must be getting better, Dixie,' Hickok noted as he hung the gunbelt over his wide shoulder. 'You look even older than the last time I set eyes on you.'

'That's cos I am.'

Dan watched both men leave the office and head in separate directions. He then saw Bobby Sanders coming across the street towards him. The youngster looked a lot better than he had the previous evening. The deputy hopped up on to the boardwalk and entered through the open doorway.

'Did I just see Pop Chance and the Circle C boys hightail it away from here, Dan?' he asked.

Dan rubbed his jaw. 'Yep.'

'Did they take Philo with them?'

'Nope.'

Sanders sat down and stared at Dan in awe. 'You must be mighty good at being a marshal! Nobody ever stood up to Pop Chance before and lived.'

Dan looked at his right hand again.

It was still shaking.

FOURTEEN

A locked door and boarded-up windows had proved no deterrent to Will Fontaine the previous night. The house on the corner of Main Street opposite the Golden Spur saloon had been exactly what the hired gun had been seeking. After a month of roughing it out on the trail with only the stars as a ceiling, even the floorboards of an empty room were luxury to Fontaine. He had slept undisturbed during the night on the top storey of the abandoned boarding-house and had only awoken when the first shafts of sunlight had managed to penetrate through the gaps in the boards nailed across the window. The gunfighter stared down from his high vantage point at the street below and watched with interest as Tom Dix came into view. Fontaine secretly observed Dix until he entered the Golden Spur.

Like all men of his profession Fontaine had heard of the man he spied upon. Although the years had

117

not been kind to Dix, Fontaine had no difficulty in recognizing him. An accidental encounter years earlier had left an impression branded into the younger man's memory that nothing could ever erase.

Men like Tom Dix were idols to those who also tried to establish themselves as men who knew how to handle their guns with lethal proficiency. Although all other hired guns were rivals to men like Fontaine, men such as Dix were different.

They did not have to try to convince folks of their renowned skills and reputation.

Perhaps it had been the pair of well-maintained guns and hand-tooled shooting rig on the veteran's hips that had first alerted Fontaine to the identity of the older gunman. It might have been the way Dix moved. For age had not altered the almost catlike walk.

The hands, unlike most peoples, did not swing back and forth in time to each stride. They remained close to the holstered gun grips in readiness.

Fontaine rubbed his cheeks with the fingers of his left hand and stood thinking. He pulled a cigar from his vest pocket, placed it between his teeth and started to chew.

Deep in thought he tried to work out why the gunfighter had entered the saloon. The very place where, he had learned, Wild Bill Hickok had rented a room.

Was there a connection?

The question troubled Fontaine.

He had not been informed that Dix was also in Gun Fury by the man who had brought him to this remote settlement to earn his blood money.

There had been tales that Dix knew Hickok. That they were friends. That both men had stood together many times and fended off all those who attempted to get the better of them. Were those stories true? Had he been brought to this place not to earn an easy payday but to be tricked for some unknown reason? He felt certain that he was good enough to get the better of the drunken Hickok in a showdown but Tom Dix was a different kettle of fish.

What if he had been hoodwinked?

Thoughtfully, Will Fontaine plucked his gunbelt off his saddle-bags and swung it around his hips. He quickly buckled up and then stooped to tie the holsters' leather laces around his pants legs. He checked that both guns were loaded and then put his hat on.

He had a man to meet. A man he knew only by name.

A man who would pay him to do the very thing he had wanted to do for most of his days.

Fontaine was going to be paid to kill the famous Wild Bill Hickok in a well-practised shoot-out. He knew that within days his name would be known from coast to coast as the man who had bettered one of the fastest guns in the West.

The gunfighter laughed to himself as he left the room and made his way down the creaking staircase towards the entrance of the empty building.

He was being paid to do something he would have willingly done for free.

Will Fontaine was going to kill a legend.

As he reached the door to the street a cold shiver raced down his spine. He paused for a moment.

A bead of sweat ran down his face.

What of Tom Dix?

Fontaine wondered if it were possible to take on two legends and survive. Was it?

He opened the door and pulled it shut behind him. He started to walk along the boardwalk. Then he realized something. Something which brought the gravity of the situation home to him hard.

He could not hear his own footsteps.

His was the walk of a dead man.

The street had been almost devoid of humanity as Dix had walked quickly along its length towards the saloon on his errand for Hickok. There had been people watching his every move though. From the corners of his eyes he had seen them hiding on either side of the street in store windows and doorways. Hiding in case Dix drew lead from Circle C guns.

Tom Dix had just entered the Golden Spur when

he saw Rufas Hardy behind the desk beside the wide staircase which led up to the rooms. The man looked tired.

'I've come for Hickok's bag,' Dix told him.

Hardy forced a smile.

'You a pal of his?'

'Yep,' Dix answered.

'Is he sober yet?'

'Getting there.'

'Wild Bill's bin no trouble really 'ceptin' for the fact that he's bin drawing gunhands like flies to a dung heap.' Hardy walked round the desk with a key in his hand and started up the flight of carpeted stairs with the gunfighter on his trail. They walked along the beautifully decorated corridor until they reached their destination. Hardy slid the key in the door lock and turned it. 'I reckon a lotta low life vermin have come to try their luck but none of them has had the guts yet. Even drunk he kinda scares most folks.'

'What happened last night?' Dix asked. 'How come he was thrown out of here?'

'Somebody told me that one of the local cowboys made fun of his girly hair,' Hardy replied. 'Bill took offence and went to pistol whip the *hombre* but he was too drunk to stand. One of the boys just picked him up and tossed him out.'

Dix said nothing as Hardy entered the room and picked up the bag from the foot of the bed. It had not even been opened since Hickok had arrived in Gun Fury. He accepted the bag and watched as Hardy locked the door again.

'How'd you stop him drinking, friend?' Hardy enquired as both men descended back to the lobby. 'I've bin trying for a month or so but he just kept on soaking it up.'

'Me and my pal locked him up in a cell,' Dix smiled. 'We figured it was the only sure way to make certain he couldn't find himself another bottle.'

'Reckon that would sober anyone up,' Hardy laughed as they reached the desk.

Dix was about to leave when the owner of the Golden Spur cleared his throat. Dix paused, looked at the man and waited.

Hardy licked his dry lips. 'Is it right that you got Philo Chance locked up as well? I had the mayor in here earlier and he was raving about it. Is it true?'

Dix nodded. 'Yep.'

Hardy looked anxious. 'Is it also right that Philo gunned down a couple of folks last night, including Cooper?'

Again Dix nodded. 'Yep.'

Hardy leaned across the desk. 'Be careful, stranger. Them Chance critters are worse than sidewinders. The only thing they won't kill is kinfolk.'

'Is Pop Chance as ornery as folks reckon?'

'Worse!' Hardy answered with feeling. 'Pop figures he owns this entire range because his family was here first. Be careful. Savvy?'

Dix continued nodding as he left the saloon and walked back out into the bright morning sunlight. He screwed up his eyes and then saw a man he had met only once a few years earlier walking toward the livery.

'Fontaine!' Dix muttered to himself.

FIFTEEN

The home of Horace Steed was bigger than most of the others within the boundaries of Gun Fury. It had been built on corrupt foundations and reflected the wealth of the man who proclaimed himself as town mayor. A decade of being a councillor had seen the one-time town clerk prosper as graft payments flowed into the pockets of those who ran the remote settlement. His pockets had flourished more than those of most people. But, as quickly as it had all started, the golden goose stopped laying its eggs when the railhead had been moved further south.

When the cattle drives had stopped coming to Gun Fury the town's fortunes evaporated with them.

Now only tumbleweed moved along the rusted railtracks at the edge of town. The remains of stock pens which had once held thousands of steers lay rotting. Most had been salvaged by those who remained in Gun Fury and were used to fuel their stoves.

The rotund man with the balding head still saw himself as the most important person in Gun Fury though. He still imagined that he alone could turn the tide and bring Gun Fury back from the brink of desolation.

He alone would be its saviour.

All it would take was an act so tremendous that the entire world would take note. He knew that other towns and places across the West had become famous because of the unplanned or even accidental actions of certain individuals.

Tombstone would have remained totally unknown to the outside world if it had not been for a brief gunfight between the Earps and the Clantons.

The Little Big Horn would have been nothing more than an array of rolling hills if George Armstrong Custer had not led the Seventh Cavalry into it.

When brutal incidents happened which caught the imagination of ordinary folks, everyone wanted to know more. To see it. To relive the unimaginable. The bloodier it was the more the public relished it.

Gun Fury required something big to happen.

Something so unexpected that it would put Gun Fury on the map for all time. Steed knew that the cattle drives would never return, but there was something else which could change the town fortunes for all time.

It had come to him like a vision.

Six weeks earlier he had stumbled across a well-thumbed dime novel in the barbershop as he had waited for his daily shave. When he had seen the cover with its crude colourful illustration of Wild Bill Hickok doing battle with a fictional foe, Steed had realized how he could make Gun Fury one of the most famous towns in the entire country.

A place where the rich Easterners would flock in droves and spend their money.

It had been far too easy to persuade Hickok to come to his town. All it had taken was a letter sealed with a couple of hundred dollars in it. Steed had borrowed the name of the writer of the dime novel. He used it as bait. Bait which had been swallowed willingly. Steed then pretended that he wanted to write a new series of stories and would meet with Hickok at Gun Fury to pay him for the use of his name and image.

Hickok had ridden a hundred miles to Gun Fury, but upon his arrival another letter awaited him at the Golden Spur. This time Steed had said that he, the writer, had been delayed. He asked Hickok to wait for him. With another hundred dollars in the envelope, Hickok was happy to do just that.

Horace Steed rested a hand on the doorframe and stared out along the almost deserted street. His was the only house remaining occupied in the eastern side of town. When he saw the man clad in black leather walking along the boardwalk towards him, Steed knew that the last part of his plan had arrived.

There was no mistaking the fancy shooting rig the man wore. This was no mere cowboy. This was a gunfighter. A gun for hire and Steed was willing to hire.

Steed rubbed his hands together gleefully. He could hardly contain his excitement.

How do you rekindle the flame of a town?

Although Will Fontaine did not realize it, he was the answer. For the gunfighter could do the one thing which would allow Gun Fury to find its place in history. The one thing which would bring fame and fortune to those smart enough to know how to exploit their town's newly found fame. Steed knew that the unsuspecting man in black who drew closer with every heartbeat held his future in the palms of his hands.

Fontaine could kill the famous Wild Bill Hickok in what Steed would ensure would become the greatest showdown of all time in the Wild West. It would be the tallest of all tall tales.

When Horace Steed had finished telling the tale to the country's newspapers, Will Fontaine would be crowned and heralded as the newest and greatest gunfighter ever to have lived.

As he approached the open doorway, Fontaine touched his hat brim and nodded.

'I'm Fontaine.'

Steed rubbed his hands and then gestured to the interior of his home. 'I'm Steed. I'm glad you arrived on schedule, Mr Fontaine.'

'I'm never late for a appointment that concerns killing someone, Steed,' Fontaine said drily. 'And when the opponent in question is one of such reputation, I spur even harder.'

'You're not afraid?' Steed asked.

'Of what?' Fontaine raised an eyebrow.

'Hickok.'

'He don't know it yet but he's already on his way to Boot Hill, Steed,' Fontaine replied. 'Besides, a man that's afraid of dying shouldn't take up being a gunfighter.'

'I've chosen well,' Steed said.

'Indeed you have.'

Both men smiled, turned and entered the large house. They would now polish the details of the mayor's ruthless plan until it gleamed like a diamond stick-pin.

The fuse had been ignited.

Philo Chance had eventually awoken from his drunken stupor and wanted everyone within Gun Fury to know it. The raging pain inside his pounding skull bore testament to the fact that the cowboy had the mother of all hangovers. He held on to the bars of his cell and shook them like the caged animal he resembled. Yet the more he rebelled, the more the pain grew. He fell to his knees and cursed.

'Let me go, you sons of bitches! Hear me? I'll kill all of you! Let me go!'

Dan Shaw glanced across from his desk at his deputy and smiled. He got to his feet, walked to the open doorway and glared into the cell.

It seemed strange to Dan. Chance was a pathetic creature in the cold light of day. Without his guns he was nothing. Just a crazed killer.

'You want some vittles?' Dan asked.

Chance swung on his knees to face the voice. He then clutched at his head and stared through bloodshot eyes.

'Open this cell.'

Dan stepped closer and rested his knuckles on his hips.

'You ain't going anywhere, Philo.'

Chance crawled on his knees towards the voice. He stared up through the bars at Dan.

'Who the hell are you?'

'I'm the new marshal, Philo,' Dan said.

'Where's Cooper?'

'You killed Cooper, Philo,' Dan replied. 'You also killed the bank teller.'

'I did?' Chance blinked hard. He rolled on to his side and rested his head against the cold bars. There were war drums pounding inside his skull and they seemed to be getting louder with every passing moment. 'Oh, yeah.'

Angrily, Dan shook his head in disgust, then took hold of the door and slammed it forcefully. The noise resounded around the building for a few seconds. He could hear the cries of the prisoner, then he walked back to his desk.

'He didn't even recall killing Cooper or Smithers, Bobby,' Dan said sadly. 'How the hell can you kill anyone and then forget about it?'

The young man looked up from his chair.

'You should have let Dix finish him off last night, Dan,' the deputy remarked. 'The chances of a jury in this town convicting him are almost zero.'

Dan stared at the deputy. 'What d'you mean?'

Sanders pointed a finger through the open office door at the sun-drenched street. He sighed heavily.

'Them folks out there are too scared of the Chances ever to find Philo guilty.'

Dan picked up his coffee cup and sipped at the hot beverage.

'If I'd let Dixie kill that rat in there what do you reckon the rest of the Circle C would do?'

'The same thing they'll do anyways, Dan.'

'What's that?'

'Punish us!'

Dan was about to speak again when he saw Dix through the window making his way along the boardwalk. Bobby Sanders looked up as Tom Dix walked into the marshal's office from the direction of the barbershop. The troubled expression etched into Dix's features drew both men's attention.

'You OK?' Sanders queried.

'What's wrong, Dixie?' Dan asked.

'I just saw Will Fontaine,' Dix answered.

'So what? Molly told us that he was in town.'

Dix rested his hands on the desk. 'I followed him for a little while.'

Sanders sat upright. 'What you do that for?'

'Curiosity.'

Dan rubbed his chin. 'Spit it out.'

'What?' Dix looked at his pal.

'What's troubling you?' Dan asked. 'Will Fontaine's just another gunman. Why are you so interested in him?'

Dix turned his attention the the deputy. 'You know that street beyond the livery, Bobby?'

'Sure enough.'

'Who lives in the real big house down there?'

Sanders raised his eyebrows. 'Old Horace the mayor. Ain't nobody else living in any of them houses down there any more, Dixie. Why?'

'Why'd you ask about the mayor's house, Dixie?' Dan wondered.

Dix looked back at Dan.

'Tell me something, old friend. Why do you reckon a hired gun would go and visit the mayor?'

131

Dan lifted his cup back to his lips and took a mouthful of the coffee. He swallowed thoughtfully.

'That's a damn good question.'

SIXTEEN

There was a vicious storm brewing high above the silent range. Black clouds had journeyed the distance between the snowcapped mountain peaks until they loomed over the remote town. There was another storm coming to the streets of Gun Fury and everyone knew it. The eerie sound of thunderclaps echoed all around. They grew ominously louder and then lightning flashed its lethal energy across the sky. Every few minutes it lit up as rippling curtains of rain rolled like stampeding herds across the dusty plains and in to the town.

But it was not the lightning which had cleared the streets and emptied most of the saloons. It was the fear of the riders who every man, woman and child knew were coming when night fell.

Every now and then a deadly rod of lightning would fork down and strike at the ground around

Gun Fury. From the marshal's office Dan Shaw had seen two strikes hit Boot Hill. He recalled the old saying that lightning never strikes twice in the same place, but he knew that it often did.

The afternoon had seemed eternal.

Nothing happened and the three men in the marshal's small office had started to become edgy. Yet for all their nerves the three remained ready for what they knew was coming.

The ranting of their prisoner had grown louder and louder as Philo Chance's drunk wore off and his head cleared. Their only consolation was that Chance's voice was starting to crack under the strain.

Darkness had spread its blanket across the town and that meant that trouble was getting closer. Each of them knew that Pop Chance would soon arrive with his sons and Circle C cowboys. This time they would not be so easily dissuaded. Dan and Dix knew that with them would come certain death.

Whose death would be left to the fickle finger of fate itself. Bobby had been about to light the office lamp when Dix raised a finger and wagged it at the deputy. The youngster sat down again and tossed the unused match aside.

Tom Dix had been in many sticky situations before but none of them had seemed to be anything like the one which faced him and his cohorts now. To face a man in a showdown was one thing he could handle with almost fearless rationality, but to wait for ruthless men to ride in at any time gnawed at his craw.

He had no idea what the Chance clan were capable of.

A lot of talk about their burning the town to the ground chilled his soul. Would they do that? If they were as mindless as Philo, he believed that nothing was beyond them. They had no qualms or morality like most folks he knew.

They believed that they had a God-given right to do what they liked without retribution. To kill without ever being brought to book. To destroy everything which stood in their way.

A bead of sweat trailed down from his stitched scalp and dripped on to his already sodden shirt. His eyes had drifted to the deputy many times during the long afternoon which had now ended. The injured Bobby Sanders had been urged many times by both of the older men to go home, but he had refused. Bobby was no quitter. Like his dead uncle he was proud of being a law officer and had that strange quality often found in men who wore tin stars.

He had grit.

Neither Dan nor Dix had mentioned it, but both were wondering where their flamboyant comrade was. It had been over seven hours since either of them had set eyes upon Hickok. Both men wondered whether the famed war hero, gunfighter and exlawman had relented over his promise to remain sober.

There were a lot of saloons in Gun Fury between the barbershop's bathhouse and the marshal's office. All of them filled with bottles of whiskey.

Dan rubbed his neck. He stepped out beneath the porch overhang and looked around at the long deserted street. The rain had dwindled to a fine shower. The sandy street was now wet and covered in places with small pools of water. He knew that that might slow the Circle C riders up a little when they eventually arrived back in town.

Dan was thankful that he had ordered the street lights not to be lit as night had come on. The darkness was another thing he prayed might help him and his friends. Without Hickok at their side they would need all the help they could get. There were just too many cowboys, he secretly thought.

Cowboys dumb enough to ignore his threat of having Philo shot dead if they attacked.

Dix came out of the office and stood by Dan's shoulder. 'We ain't got a hope in hell if we stay inside here, Dan.'

'I'm starting to think that myself, Dixie.' Dan bit his lip and found half a cigar in his vest pocket. He put it between his teeth and then fumbled for a match. 'But what can we do without moving our prisoner? We should have done something earlier.'

'I thought Hickok would have bin here before

now,' Dix sighed.

Dan shook his head. 'I reckon he got the scent of a bottle in his nostrils and has plumb forgot about us.'

'Yeah,' Dix shrugged. 'Maybe you're right.'

'I sure hope I'm not.'

'I reckon that I ought to go find a place over there.' Dixie pulled a match from his own pocket and struck its tip with his thumbnail. Dan cupped its flame and sucked smoke into his lungs. Smoke drifted from between his teeth.

Dan stared to where Dix was pointing. A narrow alley between two buildings, barely three feet wide, was plenty big enough for the lanky gunfighter to wait unseen.

'You reckon we have us a chance if we catch them in our crossfire, Dixie?' Dan blew a line of smoke at the rain.

Dix nodded and blew the match's flame out. 'Yep.'

'Are you willing to backshoot them?' Dan stared through the smoke.

'If they start shooting at this office, I'll backshoot them gladly, Dan.' Dix nodded.

'So be it! Go grab a coat and a box of shells and get over there,' Dan said firmly.

Dix did not require telling twice. He spun on his heels and moved quickly back into the dark office. He had barely reached the desk where the ammunition was kept in its deep drawers when he heard Dan curse loudly. The gunfighter rushed back to the door with Bobby at his side.

'What's wrong, Dan?' Dix asked.

Dan pulled the cigar from his mouth and pointed its smoking tip towards the end of the long street.

Dix and Bobby looked into the rain which once again was driving in great gusts. Another flash of lightning flickered its spooky illumination over the entire town once more. They both gasped at exactly the same moment. For a few brief heartbeats they saw them.

It was like watching death approaching.

The line of horsemen who had just turned into Main Street rode slowly towards their goal. Pop Chance was true to his word. He had arrived just after nightfall.

'Too late!' Dan muttered. 'They're already here!'

SEVENTEEN

Another brilliant flash of lightning lit up the town. Its bright, blinding light showed up the ten riders and the barrels of their rifles which they held aloft. It was as though none of the cowboys even noticed the downpour they were travelling through. They just continued on slowly. Then the deafening sound which resembled a dozen sticks of dynamite exploding shook the town's wooden buildings.

Bathed in the intermittent bursts of light, the rancher looked every inch the Satanic figure he truly was. Even the air had the acrid stench of sulphur as Nature's fury mocked the mere mortals upon the ground.

'We're coming to get you, Marshal!' Pop Chance bellowed out a few seconds before another deafening thunderclap resounded above them. 'Let my boy go. You hear me, lawman? You hear me? Let my boy loose!'

Using the brief moments when the town was lit up by the lurid shafts of lightning forks, Dix looked along the rest of the street. Coal-tar lanterns and lamps were being extinguished one after another as the townsfolk realized that their worst fears had arrived. He squinted hard down the long thoroughfare. Only Joe Benson's place remained defiantly illuminated. Again he thought about Hickok.

Dan kept his shoulder pressed against the doorframe. His narrowed eyes focused on the cowboys moving steadily towards them through the rain. Rain which was increasing in intensity.

'Leastways they ain't gonna burn nothing down,' Dan said coldly. 'Not in this storm anyways.'

Keeping his eyes firmly fixed on the line of horsemen, Dix drew both his Colts and cocked their hammers.

'Reckon we'll have to stay in here, boys.'

'Trapped like rats,' Dan seethed.

'I sure wish there was a back door to this place.' Bobby sighed heavily.

Dan edged back towards his men. He tossed the cigar away and pulled his own gun from its holster.

'Get all the rifles off the wall rack, Bobby,' he commanded the deputy. 'And every box of bullets you can find. This might be a long fight. If it is we'll need every damn weapon we can lay our hands on.'

'It might have bin smart if we'd stocked up with some vittles,' Dix mentioned.

'Grub's the last thing on my mind, Dixie,' Dan said.

The deputy did as he was told and scrambled away to the wall rack. His young fingers pulled the long metal link chain from between the rifles' trigger guards.

Dix leaned closer to Dan. 'Where the hell is James Butler when we need him?'

'That's just what I was asking myself, Dixie,' Dan replied. 'Say, did you tell him about that Fontaine *hombre* when you took his bag to Joe's?'

'Sure did.'

'What he say?'

'Nothing.' Dix's expression changed. 'He just lay up to his neck in a tub of soapsuds.'

'Least you warned him.' Dan bit his lip again. The two men stepped back into the relative safety of the office but remained close to the door. Their three guns were trained on the approaching riders.

As the cowboys rode past the light of the barbershop steam could be seen rising from riders and their mounts. It drifted like swirling phantoms towards the black clouds above.

'Let my Philo go and I might just let you live,' Chance shouted out again above the sound of the rain which pounded along the porch overhangs. 'Hear me, Marshal?'

'A deaf man could hear you, Chance,' Dan shouted back.

'Then do as you're told,' Chance screamed.

'Go to hell!'

Pop Chance's voice became even louder. 'It ain't me that'll be having supper with the Devil, Marshal.'

Suddenly, as yet another flash of lightning lit up Gun Fury, the seven horsemen on either side of Pop Chance and his two sons hauled rein, spurred and rode into side streets off both sides of Main Street.

'Hell! They've separated!' Dan snarled. 'Why'd they do that, Dixie?'

'Damn it!' Dix cursed. 'They must be figuring on hitting us from three directions.'

With rain beating down on them, Pop Chance led Bodine and Seth slowly on towards the marshal's office. They rode with slow deliberation through the pouring rain. Their mounts seemed barely to be walking as the cowboys eased slowly back on their reins.

Another deafening rumble shook the office as its occupants hung close to its open doorway.

'I'm kinda scared, Dan,' Bobby admitted.

'You ain't on your lonesome there, boy,' Dan sighed.

Bobby placed the rifles down close to one of the office's two windows, then went to gather up every box of ammunition he could get his hands on.

Then the prisoner piped up again from beyond the closed jailhouse door. The sound of his voice drew the attention of the three men.

'That's my pa out there!' Philo yelled out from behind them. 'Get me out of here, Pa! Teach these varmints a lesson! Kill the bastards!'

'That does it!' Dan turned and marched speedily across the office, opened the door to the jailhouse and entered. Philo Chance was still calling out with his face pressed up against the bars.

'They'll kill all of you,' Chance spat.

Without uttering a single word, Dan raised his gun and struck its grip across the the his prisoner's jaw. A loud cracking sound filled the air. Blood spilled from the cowboy's mouth. Chance fell to the floor heavily and landed in a heap. For the first time in hours he was silent.

'That's better,' Dan said as he returned to stand beside Dix and Bobby. 'I've bin wanting to do that all day.'

'Where'd you figure them cowboys went, Dan?' the deputy asked as he loaded one of the Winchesters.

Dan screwed up his eyes and stared along the dark street at the three horsemen who were getting closer. He did not answer the youngster because he was wondering exactly the same thing himself.

Then another noise above them drew the gunfighters' attention.

Dix touched Dan's arm and looked upward at the ceiling. The veteran lawman raised his eyes until they too were staring at the crude plasterwork. He

143

nodded at his pard,

'That ain't the rain,' Dix said. 'That's boots.'

'So that's where some of them stinking cowboys went, Dixie,' Dan said.

'If they block up the chimney stack we'll be choked to death in here by the smoke!' Dix remarked, pointing to the well-stoked stove.

Dan was about to reply but Dix had already run out on to the dark boardwalk. His long legs made short work of the distance towards the alley. Dan edged forward and then saw the three riders draw rein and stop their mounts. Pop Chance lowered his Winchester and fired it. The bullet cut through the rain in pursuit of the running gunfighter. A chunk of timber was torn from the wall of the side building.

Dan raised his gun and started to shoot feverishly at the mounted men.

Within seconds the cowboys had driven their horses across the street and dismounted. All three men dropped behind water troughs and then opened up. Now there was another deafening noise to equal that of the thunderclaps. Rifle bullets cut across the street into the wooden structure. The smell of burning splinters filled the nostrils of both marshal and deputy. They returned fire.

Rifle bullets shattered the two office windows. Both men were showered in thousands of glass fragments. Bobby turned and pushed the barrel of his rifle through the nearest window. He cocked its mechanism and started to fire as Dan shook the spent brass casings from his smoking gun and reloaded it.

'Keep them pinned down, Bobby,' Dan instructed.

The deputy kept firing.

Dix had reached the back of the building when he saw the three cowboy horses tied to a post. He stopped and looked up through the driving rain at the low sloping roof of the jailhouse. It protruded a foot over the back wall of building. Even above the noise of the shooting Dix could hear the cowboys moving on the shingles above him.

Dix moved between the bedraggled horses and reached the fencing that stretched twenty feet away from the building to the back alley. He could see fresh boot marks on the wood where the cowboys had climbed up the fence to get to the roof.

Dix holstered one of his weapons, then reached up until the fingers of his left hand gripped the top of the fence. With rain making his stitched-up head wound smart, he managed to pull himself up. He then pushed his left boot toe in a large knot-hole and steadied himself.

Stretching to his full height Dix peered over edge of the sloping shingles rooftop at the three cowboys. He had been correct. They were slowing moving towards the black metal chimney stack close to the front of the marshal's office. With rainwater hampering their progress and the slippery wet surface beneath their boots, they moved slowly. Cowboys were not confident at anything which took them higher than the height of a saddle.

Balancing on the fence with one hand on the edge of the roof, Dix raised his gun. He could have killed them there and then but that was not his way. It never had been.

'Howdy, boys!' Dix said.

All three cowboys were startled. They turned quickly. Dix could see that one of the bunch had a bundle of rags in one hand and a six-shooter in the other. His two fellow cowboys held on to their rifles. It was obvious to Dix what they had planned. They were going to shoot everyone who ran from the office when it filled with choking smoke.

All three raised their weapons and fired. Dix ducked and then blasted his Colt.

Faster than any of the cowboys had ever seen anyone handle a gun before, Dix cocked his gun's hammer and squeezed its trigger in rapid succession. As bullets tore at him Dix sent all six of his bullets into them. Two of the cowboys slumped forward and slid down the wet roof before crashing between their tethered horses. The third cowboy flew backwards into the air and went straight over the top of the front of the building. Dix heard him hit the porch overhang before his dead body rolled off and landed atop the hitching rail outside the marshal's office.

Dix jumped back down to the ground, swiftly

146

reloaded and then dashed towards the alley. Through the darkness and pouring rain Dix ran like a man half his actual age. He knew this was the direction in which he had last see the four other cowboys heading when they had separated from the Chances.

The shooting in the main street had paused briefly.

A startled Pop Chance had stopped chewing the plug of tobacco in his mouth when he had seen the cowboy flying over the façade and crash off the porch overhang before landing on the hitching pole.

'Damn it all!' Pop Chance cursed.

'They killed Pete, Pa!' Seth Chance exclaimed in shock.

'I heard me a whole bunch of shots, Pa,' Bodine added as he crawled closer to his father. 'I reckon they killed Jim and Red as well.'

Pop Chance pulled a handful of bullets from his coat pocket and started to push them into the rifle's magazine. His eyes burned as he stared at the marshal's office shrouded in darkness.

'They ain't gonna fight much longer! Not when the other boys come back.'

Seth leaned closer. 'What you mean, Pa?'

Pop Chance glanced at his son. 'Don't you remember the plan, Seth? What I sent Todd and the other boys to do?'

Both brothers looked at one another blankly and

then back at their father. They nodded and began to load their own rifles.

'Hell! I don't know why I bother!' Pop mumbled as the rain continued to soak them. 'Ain't a whole brain between the three of you young'uns!'

Todd Castle was top wrangler of the Circle C but he had not always wasted his energies on steers. There had been a time when he had ridden with hard-bitten gangs of outlaws. Short and bearded, Castle led the other three cowboys from their tethered mounts to the back of the hardware store.

He raised his gun, aimed at the lock and then fired. The lock shattered as the sound echoed all around the side street, but Castle knew that nobody would come to investigate.

The four men entered and made their way into the storeroom. Castle struck a match and touched the wick of a candle. As the room lit up he saw what Pop Chance had sent them to get. Two boxes on a shelf: one contained a roll of fuse wire and the other was filled with sticks of dynamite.

He waved his gun at the cowboys.

'Bring as many sticks of dynamite as you can fill your pockets with, boys,' Castle ordered them. 'I'll bring the fuse wire.'

The cowboys picked up the explosives from the box and rammed the sticks into their deep trail-coat pockets. Castle lifted the roll of wire and then led the others back towards the door.

'That's it, c'mon.'

The quartet made their way into the driving rain back to their waiting horses. After they had mounted they swung the animals around and spurred.

The four horsemen had just turned the corner and ridden into the alley when the sky lit up spectacularly. As the cowboys spurred they saw the figure running towards them. Castle dragged one of his guns from its holster and fired.

Blinded by the rain, Tom Dix was shocked. He felt the heat of the bullet as it hit him. It was like being kicked by a mule.

He was lifted off his feet by the sheer impact and thrown into a ditch.

The cowboys thundered past him.

Dix tried to get back up but it was impossible. He blinked but it did not help. He felt himself sinking into a spinning whirlpool of fevered quicksand.

A place where nightmares reigned.

The rain was easing up as Dan heard the riders galloping between the buildings just down the long, sodden street. He tried to get a glimpse of them but no sooner had he leaned a few inches out of the door when rifle fire erupted once again. He dropped on to his belly as the entire front of the marshal's office was torn to bits by yet another volley of hot lead.

'You OK?' Bobby asked.

'I bin better.' Dan lay covered in smouldering

sawdust on one side of the door as his deputy slid a rifle to him across the floor from the other. Dan grabbed the weapon and rolled away until he was underneath the other office window beside the stove. Glass littered the boards as he pushed himself up on to his knees. He felt the sharp slivers of glass cut into his knees but refused to acknowledge the pain.

More shots came at them. The back wall of the office was riddled with lead. Dan cranked the rifle's handguard and pulled its hammer back.

'I'm starting to wonder whether we've got a chance here, Bobby,' Dan blurted out.

'Don't look like it unless a miracle happens,' the youngster responded. 'And I kinda lost my faith in miracles.'

'You and me both.' Dan poked his head up and fired the Winchester through the busted window. He dropped back down as yet another volley of rifle bullets was returned.

Suddenly the shooting stopped again. The two lawmen glanced at one another through the gloom. Both knew that something was happening. Neither knew what.

Out in the street Pop Chance had seen the four cowboys stop their mounts just up from the barbershop. He crouched behind the trough and grinned a gap-toothed grin as Todd Castle waved to him.

The rancher crawled towards his bemused sons.

'Now we'll see if that ornery marshal wants to give Philo back to us, boys,' Pop Chance said.

Bodine Chance scratched his head. 'What you mean, Pa?'

The elder Chance moved to the side of the trough. He cleared his throat and shouted at the office.

'Listen up, Marshal! My boys got some real fine dynamite and they're gonna start blowing up this town building by building unless you hand Philo over!'

Dan sighed.

'What you reckon, Bobby?'

'They're bluffing,' the deputy answered.

Dan nodded. 'That's what I figured.'

'Well?' Chance shouted across the street again as he signalled to Castle. 'You still thinking that you can fight the Chance clan, Marshal?'

Before Dan could respond the largest explosion he had ever heard rocked the bullet-scarred building. A cloud of smoke and dust filled the street. It gave Dan just enough cover for him to look up the street. He gasped in horror as he set eyes on the burning remnants of a once solid building. He ducked back into the office and glanced at the terrified youngster.

'They ain't bluffing, Bobby!'

A few seconds later another massive blast sent burning debris showering down over the wide street. The smell of burning wood filled their nostrils. The dancing light of the flames in the street lit up the inside of the marshal's office.

'We oughta let Philo go, Dan.'

Dan gritted his teeth. 'Yeah. You're right, Bobby. Go unlock the cell and bring the worthless bastard here. I know when I'm beat.'

Bobby crawled quickly across the floor until he reached the back wall of the office. He stood, lifted the keys off the nail, ran into the jail and unlocked the cell door.

'He's still unconscious, Dan.'

Dan marched to the cell and picked up a bucket of water off the dirt floor. He tossed its entire contents over the pistol-whipped Philo.

The cowboy woke with a confused splutter.

Both men lifted him up, then the deputy put his shoulder under the dazed cowboy's arm and supported his weight.

'I got him, Dan,' Bobby said as he helped the staggering figure into the front office.

Dan nodded and ran back to the open door. He was about call out to Pop Chance when he saw one of the rancher's sons poke his rifle over the trough and fire it. Dan felt the heat of the bullet as it cut past him. Then he heard the deputy behind him cry out.

Dan swung his head around and saw the two men fall.

'Bobby?'

The deputy pushed the body off him and looked

back at the concerned marshal.

'I'm OK but Philo ain't.'

'Dead?' Dan asked.

The youngster nodded. 'Yep. There ain't bin a heart made that can take a bullet.'

Dan Shaw called out again. 'Who fired that shot, Pop?'

Pop Chance looked over the trough. 'What you say?'

'One of you mindless varmints just put a bullet clean through Philo, old-timer,' Dan shouted. 'Clean through his heart.'

The old man screwed up his eyes. 'You saying Philo's dead?'

'Yep. And it was one of you fools that killed him.' Dan swallowed hard as he watched Bobby crawl back to the pile of rifles.

Pop Chance sank down on to his knees. For a moment he said nothing as his eyes looked at his two remaining sons and the rifles in their hands. Then he saw the smoke trailing up from the barrel of Seth's weapon.

'You done it, Seth,' Pop growled. 'You killed your own brother, you worthless piece of dung!'

Suddenly the sound of a door being opened and closed along the street drew everyone's attention. The four cowboys with the dynamite were closest and turned around first. What they saw chilled them to the bone.

For there was no more frightening sight in the West than that of James Butler Hickok when dressed in his gunfighting clothes. He stood magnificent just outside the door of the barbershop in his long fringed buckskin coat and knee-high black boots.

His guns gleamed in the light of the inferno opposite as they waited inside the hand-tooled cross-draw shooting rig.

'Drop them fireworks and all of your guns,' Hickok ordered the four cowboys.

Castle sneered. 'Or what, Wild Bill?'

'Or I'll surely kill you.'

Without thinking the cowboys went for their guns. It was their last mistake.

Quick as a striking rattler Hickok drew both his guns and fired. It took only four bullets to drop each man in a bloody heap. With smoke trailing from the barrels of his guns, Hickok stepped down from the boardwalk and paced towards where the three Chance men were hiding.

'Drop them rifles,' Hickok demanded as he closed the distance between them. 'Unless you want to join them boys in Hell.'

'We gotta give up, Pa,' Seth pleaded.

'Seth's right,' Bodine agreed.

Defiantly Pop Chance stood up. 'Get up, you cowards! Prove to me that you're Chances. For the first time in your lives show me that you ain't yella.'

Bodine and Seth rose. The went to either side of

their father and cocked their rifles.

'Now!' Pop shouted. All three spun their Winchesters in Hickok's direction and squeezed the triggers.

The man with the long mane of hair stopped. He felt the bullets cut through his long-fringed buckskin jacket, then he cocked and fired his guns over and over until his hammers fell on spent casings.

He tilted his head and watched as Dan and Bobby ventured out of the badly damaged building.

'Wild Bill!' Dan gasped in awe.

'Where's Dixie?' Hickok asked.

Dan rubbed his neck and looked around them. His heart quickened as his mind pictured the worst.

'Oh sweet Lord!' he gasped. 'Where is Dixie?'

FINALE

Some hours later Tom Dix opened his eyes and stared around the hotel room at the blurred figures all around him. He attempted to rise but a hand on his arm held him down. As his vision cleared he saw the faces clearly. Dan and Bobby were standing behind Joe Benson. The barber was holding in one hand the bloody lead ball he had cut out of Dix's shoulder. In a corner of the room the tall, impressive figure of Hickok stood motionless.

'What happened?' Dix asked.

'You got yourself shot, Dixie,' Dan answered as the barber began to sew up the wound.

'I know that,' Dix said. 'I mean what happened with them cowboys?'

Dan glanced across at Hickok. 'Wild Bill finished them all off, Dixie.'

'I never seen such daring,' the deputy enthused. 'It was like one of them stories in the dime novels.'

Dix looked at Hickok. 'You look mighty fine, James Butler.'

Hickok smiled and then started for the door. 'Thank you kindly, old friend.'

'Where you going, Wild Bill?' Dan asked as Hickok turned the doorknob.

'I'm going to play a little poker,' Hickok replied.

The street was bathed in sunlight as Hickok walked out from the Golden Spur and inhaled deeply. He stepped down on to the still damp sand and glanced at the smouldering ashes of the two burnt-out buildings along the street. Then he saw the tall figure dressed in black. He could not make out any detail on the figure but it was clear to the experienced gunfighter that this was the man Dix had warned him about.

Will Fontaine was walking down the middle of Main Street with his coat-tails pushed over a pair of holsters. The grips of the guns gleamed in the sunlight.

Hickok walked to the centre of the street, stopped and turned his head to stare at the man.

'Fontaine?'

The man stopped with a surprised look on his face. 'You expecting me, Hickok?'

'Yep.' Hickok flexed his fingers.

Fontaine raised his hands until they were a mere two inches above the handles of his weapons. A wry smile etched itself on his face as he steadied himself.

'Go for your guns, Wild Bill!'

'Gladly, sir!' Hickok's left hand went for one of his pistols. Both gunfighters had cleared their holsters and fired on one another within a split second. The deafening sound of gunfire echoed around Main Street.

Hickok had fired only once and had then slid the gun back into its hand-tooled holster. He watched as Will Fontaine went to do the same but failed. Both guns fell from his hands. The handsome man in black looked down at his midriff and smiled when he saw the blood spreading over his shirt.

Fontaine fell face down in the sand. Hickok continued walking towards the Broken Bottle saloon. Just as he stepped up on to the boardwalk he heard Dan rush out from the Golden Spur.

'You OK, Wild Bill?'

Hickok looked himself up and down and then nodded.

'Yep. I'm feeling fine, Dan. Mighty fine! My opponent seems a little dead, though.'

Dan made his way to the body. He paused and stared down at it. He looked across at Hickok and shook his head.

'You've still got vinegar, Bill!'

'Damn right I have, old-timer!' Hickok laughed, turned to the swing doors and pushed them apart.